LONGING FOR YESTERDAY

MELISSA J. CRISPIN

Copyright © 2022 by Melissa J. Crispin

ISBN: 978-0-9600645-2-6 (print)

ISBN: 978-0-9600645-1-9 (ebook)

Published by Angry Eyebrow Press

Cover art by GetCovers

To those of you who are teetering on the edge of change and gathering the courage to take the leap:

Go for it.

Embrace it.

The best is yet to come.

Chapter One

M arlene stood in her living room and glanced around, two baby carrots in her grasp. Her beloved golden retriever was nowhere to be seen. She never dressed for work so early, and her smart dog sensed something was up from the moment they went outside in the dark.

"Who wants a treat?" Faith's nails clicked on the hardwood floors, from the opposite end of the house. She appeared by Marlene's side, lifting her chin high enough to give the saddest eyes on the planet. Marlene rested a hand on her hip. "Come on. Don't look at me like that. I have your favorite this morning."

Marlene held out her palm. The dog's ears perked up and she rushed to the doggie bed to await her reward, tail wagging. Marlene crouched to set the carrots down and patted Faith on the head while she chomped away. "Don't worry, girl. Ellen is coming by in the afternoon to check on you. You'll be used to our new routine in no time." She straightened, grabbed her car keys, and headed out the door.

A new year, a new job. Life would be different, but this time, it would be a change Marlene sought out, and not one that came out of nowhere and crushed her.

But, before she took on a brave, new world, she needed a caffeine boost. She yawned as she pulled into Murray's, a popular coffee shop in town. Bells jingled and the glorious smell of fresh baked pastries filled her nose as she stepped through the entrance. Pine garland and red bows hung from the walls. The place bustled with activity. An employee took down a *Happy Holidays* banner in the far corner. Many of the tables were occupied. Some clicked away on laptops or read the paper, while others sat in small groups and talked.

A young woman stood at the counter, her dark hair tied back in a bun. She held a tray as she transferred croissants and muffins into the glass case beside her. "Good morning. How can I help you?"

"Hi. I'll have a large coffee, please. Cream, no sugar," Marlene said.

"Is there anything else I can get you?" The woman asked.

Everything. Marlene wanted to eat all of the things. It would be a dangerous, albeit delicious habit to fall into, though, eating pastries every morning on her way to work. She opted to stay strong, lamenting over a chocolate croissant on the inside. "No, thank you."

"Alright." The woman set down the tray and prepared the order. "That will be two dollars and twelve cents, please."

Marlene thanked her, paid for the coffee, and turned for the door. She paused to let another person inside, her mouth falling open as the man's midnight blue gaze locked on hers. She took a small step back. "Brady?"

Brady's brows knitted together as he pushed away dirty blond locks that nearly fell into his eyes. He sported a five-o'clock shadow that outlined his high cheekbones and the chiseled edge of his jaw. A black jacket stretched across his broad shoulders. Even through all the layers, Marlene could detect the outline of a lean, firm body.

Damn. Of course, he still looked good enough to lick. Marlene certainly didn't divorce him for being ugly.

"Marlene? You're out and about early," Brady said. Based on her old schedule, she'd still be roaming the house in her pajamas, which was no secret to her ex-husband. No harshness coated his tone, and no tension emanated in his stance, only what seemed to be a hint of surprise.

Marlene faked considerable interest in adjusting the plastic lid of her cup. Why did he have to be friendly, on the rare occasions they bumped into each other? If he acted like an ass, she'd be less likely to imagine throwing her arms around his neck and pulling him down for a kiss. Not that it mattered. He was never around when they were married, so no amount of lingering affection for him negated that fact.

"Yeah. Heading out to Warren. I'm starting work at a new company."

He tilted his head. "Really? That's over an hour away. I thought you loved your job."

Marlene shrugged one shoulder. "Time to move on."

Brady's face tightened. Marlene sensed the concern radiating off him, but she didn't need his pity or anyone else's.

"So, what brings you back to Mistport?" Deflection. Both an art form and a necessity for Marlene to operate in her small town. Two topics always came up, as if on repeat. Everyone either gave their condolences about her little brother Noah and his wife Tracy's tragic accident, or they told her what a shame it was that she and Brady couldn't work things out. While they may have had their hearts in the right place, Marlene hated rehashing the past with people who weren't even close to her.

He shoved his hands in his coat pockets. "I'm helping out Scott through his busy season." He flashed open one side of his jacket, revealing a blue shirt with a white emblem for his brother's oil delivery company, Nice Guy Oil.

Marlene noted his choice of words. Through busy season only—as in not here for good. Some things never changed.

"Trina is pregnant with triplets and on bed rest," he continued.

"Is she okay?" Marlene liked her ex-sister in law, but keeping in touch proved mega awkward. They had grown distant, but Marlene still wished the best for her.

"Yeah, she's nearing the end of her pregnancy and the doctor recommended she take it easy as a precaution."

"I'm glad it's not serious." She hesitated, not wanting to leave, but not understanding why either. "I've got to go, Brady. Take care."

His attention dropped to her lips, the way it used to right before he kissed her. Marlene's heart stuttered.

"You too." Brady held the door open for her. The woodsy scent of his cologne caught in her nose as she brushed past him. She ignored the tingling sensation from the faint contact. It wasn't like she got to enjoy his physical presence when they were together. She couldn't smell or touch a person who left her for three to twelve months at a time.

Yet another compelling reason to start over again.

Chapter Two

B rady walked into Nice Guy Oil and placed a coffee on Scott's desk. His brother pressed the phone to his ear with one shoulder, as he pulled up a customer's records on the screen in front of him. He scheduled an oil delivery and hung up.

"Guess who I bumped into at Murray's," Brady said, settling in at Trina's workspace across the room from Scott.

Scott snorted. "That's easy. Marlene. Thanks for the coffee, by the way." He held up his cup in a mock toast.

"Am I that obvious?" Brady fired up the computer.

"Kind of. No one rattles you the way she does." Scott took a sip of his drink. "How's she doing? Holding up okay?"

Brady crossed his arms and waited for his email to load. "I tried to ask, but she shut me down. You know, Marlene."

"She'd let the sky open up and swallow her whole before she talked about Noah's death. Not that I blame her." Scott shook his head.

Brady's chest constricted. Marlene had raised her younger brother, Noah, after her parents died in a terrible car accident. To lose Noah, in the same way, so soon after Brady and Marlene divorced, the thought made him want to puke.

A lump formed in his throat. He loved Noah like a brother, and the reality of never seeing him again still seemed impossible. How did she deal with all of it?

"Such a shame, you had to be a selfish idiot and lose Marlene. Trina and I miss hanging out with her."

Leave it to Scott to lighten the mood with an insult. Brady rolled his eyes. "Sorry if my divorce ruined things for you guys. I'll keep you in mind for my next relationship." Not that he wanted to entertain the idea of anyone but Marlene as his wife.

"Now you're talking. Make sure they're good aunt material, too. We need reliable babysitters." Scott laughed.

Brady crumpled up a piece of paper and hurled it at Scott's face.

"In all seriousness, why not tell her you want her back?" Scott asked. "You do, don't you?"

"When a woman asks for a divorce, that's a solid sign they're done with you." Brady scrubbed a hand over his face.

"Tell her you're not teaching abroad anymore."

Brady's jaw clenched. "Drop it, man. This conversation is pointless."

"What are you going to do when you bump into her one day, and she's with someone else?"

The image made Brady see red. He curled his hand into a fist. "Shut up, Scott. You have triplets on the way. Why don't you worry about you?" Brady's cell phone rang. He never picked up unknown numbers, but he made an exception in the name of getting Scott to shut the hell up. "Hello?"

"Is this Brady Miller?" a woman asked on the other end of the line.

"Yes, this is Brady."

"Hi, my name is Sylvia and I'm calling from the JET Program. We received your application and would like to invite you to interview for a position in Tokyo this summer."

Brady glanced at his brother and turned away from him. "An interview?"

Scott muttered something unintelligible.

"Can you come to the Japanese Embassy in New York City on Monday, February fifth at one o'clock?"

Brady's shoulders hunched. "Thank you for the opportunity, but I'm no longer available."

"I'm sorry to hear that," Sylvia said. "If you're interested at a later date, you'll need to resubmit an application."

"I understand. Thanks again." Brady hung up and went back to the paperwork sitting on his desk.

After a stretch of silence, Scott cleared his throat. "If you want to take another contract, Trina and I will figure it out. I appreciate what you're doing, but I don't want to hold you back, if it's what you really want."

Brady pursed his lips. His brother's mood swings could give a guy whiplash. He had been talking about staying put and chasing Marlene before the call. The exact opposite of pursuing another teaching position in a different country. Whatever. All Scott's worrying about the triplets, Trina, and the business she helped run like a top probably had him in a fog.

Even if Tokyo was the number one place he wanted to teach next, he wouldn't feel right leaving. Scott and Trina needed help from a person they could trust. They had tried hiring a new guy, then promptly fired him when money started disappearing. It was an extra headache Scott didn't need. Besides, the two of them supported him through the divorce and kept him in one piece, and this was a chance to give back to them.

"The job at Mistport Elementary has the discounted childcare you need, and you know it. I promised I would help and I'm sticking to my word."

Scott popped his chin up at Brady. "Thanks."

Brady shook his head. "Don't mention it. What are brothers for?"

Chapter Three

Marlene sat down at the round table in the conference room. Her orientation with the woman in HR ended early, so she had a few minutes before her boss and the rest of the team showed up.

She opened her notebook and tapped her pen against the paper, reviewing her notes from the prior meeting. A list of documents she needed to fill out for payroll and benefits stared back at her.

The words blurred on the page, her mind drifting to the coffee shop. She hadn't seen Brady since Noah's funeral, but she thought of him more often than she cared to admit to herself. So many times she wanted to crumple into his arms and have him tell her everything would be okay. The nights she lay in her bed alone sobbing, she reminded herself he wasn't even in the country, probably off in South America or Asia somewhere teaching kids how to speak English. His itch for adventure and culture trumped how he felt about her.

He loved her. She never doubted that. He just loved himself more.

Two women entered the room, engaged in a conversation about the latest episode of *The Bachelor*. One of them was tall and slender with long, blonde hair. The other seemed average height with wavy, red locks and deep set green eyes.

"Hi, you must be Marlene," the blonde said. She pulled out the chair beside Marlene and sat down. "I'm Paige."

"And I'm Sierra," the other woman said.

"Hello. Nice to meet you," Marlene said.

"Glad to see you're getting to know each other." Her new boss, Carlos, breezed in and settled at the table. "How's the first day been so far?" He exuded the same calm, friendly demeanor she had picked up on during the interview.

Marlene smiled. "Good, thanks."

"Excellent. I wanted to discuss what needs to be completed over the coming months." He turned to Marlene. "Paige and Sierra are transferring to the San Diego office when it opens in the spring, too. You'll be working closely now and especially when you move. How does that sound?"

Sounded great. New people to work with, and a new place to live, far, far away. Once she worked up the nerve to tell her neighbor and best friend, Ellen, she would be gone soon, the final weight would be lifted from her shoulders and she could start over.

"Perfect." Marlene flipped to a blank page. "Let's do it."

Carlos gave a rundown of existing accounts in the bay area, assigning them to one of the women as he went. He had started selling the company's software on the west coast a year ago, and business had grown enough to justify opening a satellite office.

"I expect each of you to keep your respective clients happy. Follow up with them on a regular basis. Offer support and answer questions. Gain a sense of what they might need, so you can sell them more products." Carlos leaned back in his chair and crossed his ankle over his knee. "The training division will be sending you a tips and tricks document for winning clients in a new region. Francesco, head of training, will be your point person for any questions that come up."

"I researched prospects in the area," Paige said. "We could split it up and cold-call them."

Carlos nodded. "Please do. Can I trust you and Sierra to show Marlene the ropes?"

"Of course," Sierra answered.

Carlos stood. "I'm sorry to leave so soon, but I'm running late and I don't want to miss my flight to London. I'll check in tomorrow. Welcome to the team, Marlene." He shook Marlene's hand and exited the room.

Marlene walked back to her desk with her new co-workers. They sat in the same area, their cubicles clustered together. Paige and Sierra rolled their chairs over to Marlene and took turns showing her the ins and outs of the various systems.

"So, are you excited to be moving soon?" Sierra asked Marlene.

They had finished the training session and both she and Paige had returned to their desks.

"You have no idea," Marlene said, an image of Brady flashing in her mind.

"I bet we do," Paige cut in. "If I'm ever going to find a man, I need to get the hell out of here."

Marlene's brows furrowed. Paige was gorgeous, and she seemed to have a great personality. Marlene would have imagined men falling over themselves to get to know her.

"Paige, Marlene's first day may not be the time for you to tell her crazy stories about you."

Paige sighed. "Fine. I'll withhold for now." One side of her mouth kicked up. "No promises on tomorrow though."

Sierra laughed. "You are so weird sometimes." She turned to Marlene. "Please excuse us. We've worked together for a long time. We know way too much about each other."

Marlene smiled. "No worries." She took their easy banter as a promising sign she would like the new place.

"Do you want to come out for a drink after work?" Sierra asked.

Her stomach tensed. Drinks would lead to chit chat about herself. She wasn't ready to talk about her screwed up life. They weren't pitying her at the moment, and she wanted to keep it that way.

"I would love to, but I can't tonight. My commute is long, and I need to head home to take care of my dog. She's not used to being home alone for so long."

At least it was partly true. Ellen would've been more than happy to let Faith out again.

"We understand. Maybe some other time?" Paige asked.

"Definitely."

Chapter Four

B rady sat at a small table in the corner of Murray's with a tablet in one hand. He read about Tokyo on his favorite travel blog, jotting down places he would've visited, if he hadn't turned down the interview. The exercise was pointless but made him appear busy in the crowded café.

He yawned and reached for his extra-large cup of coffee. He appreciated Scott and Trina's free room and board while he searched for an apartment, but witnessing their non-stop love fest didn't always sit well.

Last night, murmurs and soft laughter from their bedroom had drifted down the hall. Picturing them laying around having a grand old time grated on Brady's last nerve. He had closed his door and attempted to go to sleep, but ended up tossing and turning for hours.

There was a time when Brady and Marlene barely fought, or, whenever they did, it seemed worth it, so they could make up afterward. Even now, he couldn't quite figure out where they went wrong. As if on cue, Marlene walked into the coffee shop and placed an order. She glanced his way and did a double take when their eyes met. Brady waved. She flashed a tight smile and turned back toward the counter.

Yes. She was done with him. And even though Brady was researching the next country he wanted to live in, he didn't feel done with her.

He willed himself not to stare at her, to ignore the way her belted, buttoned-up peacoat accentuated the curves of her body.

Beyond the physical attraction, he itched to know her again. What did she do in her free time? Did she still enjoy watching terrible chick flicks, or had she moved on to a different movie genre? How was the new job treating her? Was the commute as terrible as it seemed? Seeing her nearly every weekday for the last two months yielded a growing interest in her, one that showed no signs of diminishing any time soon.

Marlene grabbed her coffee and spun around. She fumbled with an earring and peeked in his direction before walking out the door. Brady rested his elbow on the table and covered his mouth.

The small, familiar gesture meant more to him than it probably should. Back in college, she had stolen looks at him this way before they met, fueling him with the courage to introduce himself and ask her out on a date. Even throughout their marriage, he would catch her doing it in the car or while they watched TV.

Was it a sign or just an old habit yet to be broken? Tomorrow seemed as good a day as any for Brady to find out.

Chapter Five

M arlene stepped into the elevator and pressed the button for her floor, hanging her head low. She couldn't believe her luck, or lack thereof. Only she would divorce someone for not being around, and then start bumping into that person on the regular. Murray's had always been her go-to spot for coffee, not Brady's. She gripped the straps of her leather tote tighter and navigated through the cubicles. All she needed to do was wait him out. Once Trina popped out those babies, he would leave again, like he always did. But when the hell was that?

"Not soon enough," she muttered under her breath, as she placed her bag down on her desk.

"What's that?" Paige spun her chair around, her fingers curled around a black mug that said *Of course I talk to myself, I'm the funniest person I know* in bold white letters.

"Nothing. Sorry." Marlene hadn't realized she was speaking out loud. "How's the coffee here?"

"Terrible, but it's the right price. Free." Paige laughed. "I'm keeping to a strict budget so I can buy fabulous, new things when I get my butt to San Diego. A new bedroom set, kitchenware, a giant TV, you name it. I can't wait."

Marlene huffed a sigh. "Tell me about it."

"Are you okay?"

Marlene shifted under Paige's gaze. She had gotten to know Paige and Sierra over the last two months, and she liked them. Maybe it was time to open up. She couldn't develop a real friendship if she hid everything about herself.

"I'm fine, but I'd be better if my ex-husband would stop popping up at my favorite coffee shop. I mean, when we were married, he was constantly out of the country. Now that we're not, I see him almost every morning." She pressed her palm to her forehead. "He makes me crazy."

"I see." Paige shook her head. "You might like the coffee here after all."

"Sorry if that's T.M.I." Marlene plopped down in her chair and faced Paige.

Sierra came around the corner; her laptop bag slung over one shoulder. "Are you kidding? Paige is the queen of oversharing." She smirked.

Paige shrugged. "Guilty as charged. I have an idiot ex, too, so you're not alone."

Marlene glanced between both women. They lacked the sympathetic faces she had grown accustomed to whenever Brady came up in conversation. Not knowing him personally made all the difference. What a relief.

"We really need to go out for happy hour," Sierra said. "How about tonight?"

Marlene hesitated. The forecast called for snow. Considering both her parents and Noah died in car accidents, she wasn't too keen to risk it. She didn't want them to think she was an anti-social freak, though, so instead of simply declining, she would counter for a change. "Did you hear a storm is coming? How about tomorrow?"

"It is?" Sierra asked. "Screw that, then. Any night this week works for me. I hate driving in the snow." She smiled. "We won't be worrying about that in San Diego now, will we?"

Marlene chuckled. "I guess not."

A few hours later, Marlene glanced out the window near her desk. The weather had turned earlier than expected. Fat snowflakes fell from the gray sky, sticking to the roads and sidewalk. A plow truck cleared the parking lot below.

Her stomach grumbled. Unfortunately, there was no cafeteria in the building, so Marlene had to head outdoors if she wanted lunch. The deli across the street made good sandwiches and the walk would be quick. She sighed, turning to her closet to grab her coat, hat, and gloves.

"Are you venturing out for food?" Paige asked.

"Yeah. I considered not eating to avoid the snow, but that's not happening."

Paige flashed a grin. "The more I get to know you, the more we have in common. I'm coming with. Hang on." She shrugged into her leather jacket.

"Can you grab me a salad with grilled chicken?" Sierra asked.

Marlene opened her mouth to say yes, but Paige beat her to an answer. "Absolutely not. You want lunch? Brave the cold like the rest of us."

Sierra's eyes widened. "You're so mean. I have a two-hour conference call, remember?"

Marlene froze as the two women stared each other down. Awkward.

"Come on," Sierra continued. "Do me a solid. A girl's gotta eat." She folded her hands together.

After a stretch of quiet, Paige cracked a smile and Sierra snorted. The tension in Marlene's shoulders ebbed. She exhaled.

"We'll be back with your salad." Paige crinkled her nose on the last word.

"We can't all be tall, skinny blondes." Sierra reached for her purse and handed a twenty-dollar bill to Paige.

"Whatevs. Guess who's grabbing me lunch when the next storm rolls around?"

Sierra shook her head.

Paige tapped a finger on her chin. "I think I'll wait for heavy rain to cash in on my favor."

Marlene and Paige stepped outside into the bitter cold. Wind blew in their direction, launching wet snowflakes straight at their faces. They sloshed through the un-shoveled walkway.

"Brr," Paige said. "Sierra so owes me for this."

A layer of freezing rain had fallen before the snow, making each step a challenge to stay upright.

"So, what's the story with your ex-husband?" Paige asked.

Marlene let out a loud breath. "It's a long one."

"Oh? Mine's quick so how about I go first?" Paige crammed her hands in her pockets. "My ex hated his horrible boss, who supposedly forced him to work late all the time. One night, I made dinner and surprised him at the office, and I received the shock of my life instead."

Marlene gasped. "You caught them?"

Paige nodded. "Next thing I knew, I was cursing at him and hurling a container of chicken parm at his head, while he tried to explain himself. It split open on contact, red sauce and cheese exploding all over their naked bodies. To this day I can't unsee the whole thing." She shuddered. "It's as gross as it sounds. You?"

Poor Paige. At least Brady didn't cheat on her, or rather, she didn't think so. They stopped at the crosswalk and waited for the traffic light to turn red. Marlene took a deep breath and prepared to spill her guts. If Paige could share why her marriage didn't work out, so could she.

"Brady and I started dating in college. I had seen him around and thought he was cute, so when he asked me out, one morning in the commuter parking lot, I said yes. Those early years were good times." A hollow ache formed in her chest. If only they could go back.

"You didn't live in the dorms?" Paige asked.

"I couldn't. I was raising my little brother, Noah. My parents died in an accident when we were young."

Traffic cleared and they crossed the street.

"That's terrible. I'm sorry," Paige said.

"Thanks. That was a long time ago, so I've made peace with it, but losing Noah last year"—she closed her eyes a brief moment— "not so much." She swallowed past the lump in her throat. "Sorry. This is supposed to be about the ex, right?"

Paige stopped walking, now in front of the deli. Her mouth dropped open. "I'm rarely at a loss for words. I'm so sorry, Marlene. Why didn't you say anything to us?"

Marlene sighed. "So you wouldn't look at me like that."

Paige averted her gaze and reached for the door. "I can't begin to imagine what that's like for you."

They ducked inside.

"It's okay," Marlene said, even though it wasn't. What else could she say? "So my marriage fell apart, before Noah passed. Brady wanted to see the world. Experience new cultures, see how different people live."

They walked up to the young guy behind the counter. He stared at Paige as her eyes roamed the menu, but she didn't seem to notice. They each ordered a sandwich and Sierra's salad and stood off to the side to wait.

"So, what happened with you two?" Paige asked. "Did he want to blow all your money traveling nonstop?"

"No. He's a teacher, and he gets contracts to live in different countries to teach English as a second language for several months at a time. He would leave me and Noah at home, go off and do his thing, then come back. I'd be there waiting around." She shook her head. "Like a piece of furniture. We grew apart."

Paige sighed. "That sucks. Who broke it off?"

"I did. He kept pushing for me to go with him on an assignment in Italy and I lost it. I couldn't stand being pushed anymore, you know?"

"Italy sounds romantic." A faraway look crept into Paige's facial expression.

"Whose side are you on?" Marlene lifted a brow.

"Sorry," she mumbled. "I've never left the country, but I have a list. Italy's at the top. You didn't want to go?"

Marlene shrugged. "Sure, I did, but I couldn't leave Noah. We got into a huge fight. Brady accused me of being a martyr. I told him he was selfish and never considered what I wanted. To quote my brother, we just didn't want the same things in life."

Paige pressed her lips together and nodded. The guy came over and handed Paige the bag, containing their order, and telling her to come back soon. Marlene resisted the urge to roll her eyes. They trudged back out into the cold. The snow had picked up the pace.

They walked along, approaching the crosswalk with careful, measured steps. An enormous, white SUV attempted to slow at the intersection. The tires locked, but the vehicle barreled forward, skidding on the sheet of ice that coated the road. It hopped the curb, heading straight for Marlene and Paige.

Marlene shoved Paige out of the way. A sickening crunch reverberated in her ears and a burst of pain erupted in her leg. She hurtled into the air then slammed down hard on the pavement, head first. Her eyelids fluttered, but she couldn't open her eyes. Paige screamed, but Marlene couldn't tell where she was. Darkness tugged her into a deep sleep.

Chapter Six

Brady saved the Profit and Loss statement he had been working on, and then pulled the ringing cell from his pocket. Marlene's name flashed on the screen. A light-hearted feeling spread through him. What he picked up on earlier that morning had not been his imagination. He clicked *Accept* and pressed the device to his ear. "Hello?"

"Is this Brady?" asked a strange female voice.

"Who's this?" His brows creased. "And why are you calling me from Marlene's phone?"

"I'm Paige, a friend of hers from work," she said, a sob following her introduction. Brady's blood went cold. His fingers gripped the edge of his desk. "There's been an accident and she's at Warren Hospital. She's told me you're divorced. Her phone was unlocked and I didn't recognize any other names in her address book. Does she have family I can contact?"

Bile rose in Brady's throat. "No. Just me. Is she okay?" Paige's shaky breaths made his heart beat faster.

"She's...hurt, but nothing life threatening. Would you be willing to come visit her?"

His chest constricted. Did Marlene doubt him? "Of course. Did she ask for me?" A long pause followed. "Paige?"

"Yes, she did. Meet me in the waiting area on the second floor."

Brady's mouth slackened. "Why?"

"Because you need to know a few things before you see her. Please get here quick." Paige hung up.

His stomach rolled as her words sunk in. He grabbed his keys and shot up from his seat.

"Where are you going?" Scott called out, but Brady was already out the door and running to his truck.

Brady cursed at every car on the road, his fingers clenched around the steering wheel. The other drivers were exercising caution in the bad weather, but he didn't have time for that. He needed to get to the hospital.

Please let her be okay.

He rushed to the designated meeting spot when he finally arrived. The hairs on the back of his neck had risen when she made him promise not to go straight to Marlene's room. Why not? He had a right to—to what exactly? He didn't have a right to anything as far as Marlene was concerned and he damn well knew it. Since Marlene probably instructed Paige to talk to him first, he complied. He would play by her rules in hopes that she would let him back into her life.

A handful of people milled around, but one person sat in a corner by herself. The puffy-eyed blonde woman stared at the floor, seeming to be in a daze.

He walked over to her. "Are you Paige?"

The woman's gaze lifted. "Brady?"

He nodded. His throat went dry as he took in the grim twist of her mouth. "Is Marlene okay? Where is she?"

Paige sucked in a deep breath, her shoulders lifting and then lowering as she exhaled. "She's in room 2595." Brady turned to head down the hallway, but Paige stood and grabbed his arm. "Wait."

His brows shot up and he dropped his attention to her hand. Marlene lay in a hospital bed, asking for him, and this woman he met sixty seconds ago wanted him to wait? Hell no.

"Please," Paige added. "It's important."

If not for Paige calling, he wouldn't be aware of anything going on with Marlene. He scrubbed his face with both hands and sat beside her. "What happened?" he asked.

"We were walking down the road on our way back to the office. A car lost control and jumped on the sidewalk. Marlene pushed me out of the way before I could react. The car hit her."

A wave of nausea rolled through Brady. Could this be worse than he imagined? Paige had mentioned an accident on the phone, but he envisioned them in the damn car.

Paige rubbed her hands on her pants. "She flew backward from the impact and smacked her head on the pavement hard. I called 911 and tried to keep her conscious, but she passed out before the ambulance got there."

Brady was glad he sat down before she started talking because his legs would've given out. Losing Marlene was his biggest regret to date. He almost lost her for good.

"Can I go to her now? Why are you out here?"

Paige bit her bottom lip. "She doesn't remember me."

His mouth fell open. "What?"

"I was sitting by her bed when she came to, and she asked me two questions. The first one was, 'Who are you?'" Paige shook her head.

Knots formed in his stomach. "And the second?" Brady asked.

She turned her head to meet Brady's gaze. "Can you call my husband? He must be worried sick."

Chapter Seven

Marlene lay back against her pillow and stared up at the doctor. The words coming out of his mouth couldn't possibly be true. Didn't people with amnesia forget everything? She still knew her name, address, and birthday. Wouldn't she have forgotten such important facts? "There must be some kind of mistake," she said.

"I'm afraid not," he said. "You have no recollection of the event that brought you here, and you didn't recognize the woman who came with you in the ambulance. According to her, you're co-workers."

She frowned. The stranger sitting beside her earlier had seemed distraught. Were they friends?

"What's today's date, Marlene?"

Marlene bit her bottom lip. "January twenty-second, twenty-fifteen?"

The doctor gave a small shake of his head. "Today is March third, twenty-seventeen."

All the air rushed out of her lungs. Two years had vanished from her brain. He flashed an apologetic smile. "I'm sorry, Ms. Martin. We're keeping you for observation, but you'll be discharged tomorrow. We'll provide a pair of crutches for you and a recommended list of neurologists for follow-up." He stood. "With time, your memories may come back, but please prepare yourself to accept that they might not." He nodded and walked out of the room.

She focused on the ceiling, concentrating on her breathing. Deep breath in, deep breath out. Once she gained composure, she could start calling everyone, starting with Noah. There was a six-hour time difference in Prague, so she would wait until later to call Brady—except maybe he wasn't in Prague anymore. His assignment would've been long over by now.

Someone knocked on the hospital door.

"Come in," she said. Brady entered the room. The tightness in her belly loosened. "Thank God you're here. I didn't want you to worry."

Brady rushed to the bed, stopped short, and took a small step back. "I came as soon as I heard." He settled in the chair beside her, clasping his hands in his lap.

Alarm shot through her aching body. The distance between them seemed like miles. She wanted to lose herself in his arms, but he wouldn't even touch her. What was going on?

"Paige, your friend from work, called me from your cell." He reached into his coat pocket and handed Marlene the phone. "She said you pushed her out of the way, before getting hit by that car. She's pretty shaken up. I told her to head home and rest, but you should probably call her at some point."

The stiffness in Brady's demeanor hurt more than her injuries. "I—I don't know her," Marlene said after a long pause. "When did you get back from Prague? Why are you all the way over there?"

Brady frowned. His eyes met hers. "Don't you remember what happened while I was there, Marlene?"

She swallowed. "The doctor diagnosed me with retrograde amnesia. The last two years of my memory are gone."

Brady rubbed the back of his neck.

"He said there's a chance it might come back." Marlene smoothed the sheets over her legs, sparing a glance at the right one. It was wrapped in a cast and elevated, creating a larger lump beneath the covers on that side. Brady leaned forward, resting his elbows on his knees. He opened his mouth, then closed it.

"What is it, Brady?"

His brows creased. "I'm not sure where to begin. Get a little sleep. I'll come back tomorrow, and then we can talk about everything."

As his words settled in, unease embedded in her gut and spread through her body, down to her toes.

"You'll come back tomorrow?" she repeated. Her mind traveled back to the time she was hospitalized for dehydration and he had glued himself to her side. After being hit by a car he wasn't staying with her? He had always been protective. At least he had been whenever they were in the same zip code. It made no sense.

He nodded and rose from his seat.

"Brady, what the hell's going on? You're scaring me."

His lips went thin. "Everything's fine. Let's drop it for now."

Her cheeks heated. "Stop treating me like I'm ten. You're keeping something from me. Sit down."

Brady dropped back into the chair, his shoulders slumped. "Try to stay calm, okay?"

Marlene crossed her arms. The longer he held back, the less patient she grew.

He met her gaze. "We're divorced."

"What? No." Her heart raced, the monitors attached to her body beeping in warning.

He touched her arm. "It was amicable. We didn't fight over who got what. We just went our separate ways."

She shook her head. "Is this some kind of joke? This isn't funny."

Brady let out a bitter laugh. "Trust me. It's neither of those things."

She picked up her cell and searched through her contact list for Noah. He would tell her what was happening. In fact, why hadn't she called him yet?

"What are you doing?" Brady lunged for her phone, his face turning pale.

She twisted away. "Why do you care, seeing as we're divorced?" Noah wasn't in her contacts, which seemed odd, but he didn't need to be. She would never forget his number. Her fingers flew over the keypad and she hit send.

"The number you have dialed is not in service. Please check to make sure you have the right number in mind, then try again," A robotic female voice said on the line.

Marlene pulled the phone away from her ear, and studied the digits for the unsuccessful call. They seemed correct. She tried once more, this time slower. Had she forgotten even more than the doctor thought she did?

The same message repeated itself. Brady took the device and set it aside. A slight chill crawled up her spine.

"Where's Noah?" Marlene asked.

Brady placed his head in his hands. "I really don't think we should do this right now, Marlene. We may be divorced, but that doesn't mean I don't care about you. Let it go."

Every muscle in her body tensed. "Tell me. Please."

Brady never cried. Not ever. So when their gazes collided and tears spilled from his eyes, she fell to pieces.

"What aren't you telling me?" Her voice shook.

He reached for her hand and squeezed. "I'm sorry. I'm so, so sorry, Marlene. He's gone."

Chapter Eight

B rady climbed into his pickup, in the hospital parking garage and shut the door. He shivered, but the below-freezing temperature had little to do with it. Leaving Marlene gutted him, but she didn't ask him to stay. He hated the idea of her being alone.

He turned the key in the ignition and called Marlene's best friend and neighbor, Ellen. Of course, he and Ellen had been neighbors, once upon a time, too. She didn't like him much and couldn't have cared less about showing it. When he caught wind of the accident, he asked Ellen to take Marlene's dog, Faith, to her house overnight. She immediately said yes, but she wanted him to keep her updated.

"What took you so long?" Ellen answered in favor of hello. "I've been freaking out over here."

"Hi, Ellen," Brady said. "Sorry."

"Well? Is she okay? What happened?"

He paused. Ellen annoyed the hell out of him, but she was a loyal friend to Marlene, always there for her through all the crazy stuff that went on. He considered how to describe Marlene's current state.

He gave her the rundown, and when he got to the part about Marlene not remembering the divorce, Ellen shrieked.

"I couldn't believe it either," he said. "She's getting released tomorrow and I'll be bringing her home. Are you busy in the morning? Can you come with me to pick up her car at her office? We can ride over together and then one of us can drive it home."

Silence stretched. "Ellen?"

"Um, yeah. I can help, no problem, as long as it's after the kids are off to school. Brady?"

His brows knitted. "Yes?"

"Does she remember Noah and Tracy's accident?" she asked, her tone etched with concern.

He sighed. "No. She started to call him and when the number was disconnected, well, I had to explain. I didn't want to, but—"

"She insisted, I'm sure. I get it," Ellen said. "She's probably going to need help when she gets home. Maybe I can convince her to stay in my spare bedroom."

Brady scoffed. "Not likely. Don't worry, though. I'm going to take care of her." He meant it. No way was he leaving her to fend for herself injured and confused.

"Is that so?" A hint of sarcasm came through in Ellen's voice. "Are you sure you don't have a compelling assignment to run off to?"

"Ellen, can we put our differences aside for the time being? I'm exhausted, and I want to do the right thing."

"Fine." Ellen didn't sound convinced. "Then promise you won't break her heart again."

Well wasn't that the pot calling the kettle black?

Brady helped Marlene into the truck. She had barely said anything since he arrived at the hospital. Her silence made him uncomfortable, so he found himself spewing words. He began with the essentials, bringing her up to speed on the whereabouts of her car and her dog.

Her face crumpled at the mention of Faith, who had been Noah and Tracy's pet first, or their child as they always referred to her. He wanted to punch himself.

"I'm sorry," he said.

"Don't be," she whispered. "I just don't know what to make of all this. I'm very confused."

"It's a lot to take in."

"Why are you being so nice to me if we're not together?" she asked.

Because he never stopped loving her, even after she tossed him out of her life. He had been pushing for them to go abroad, so Marlene could experience new things. She had accused him of making her choose between him and Noah, but she misunderstood. Noah was getting older and wiser with a sensible head on his shoulders, thanks to her. He would've been fine. Brady wanted her to travel with him, for her and her alone. She never had the chance to do anything for herself, and she deserved everything in life. Their marriage fell apart on a mistake that he didn't fight hard enough to explain. He was an idiot.

"Being mean would serve no purpose either." Brady pulled away from the curb. "Are you sure you don't want to take Ellen up on her offer to stay with her for a while?"

She glanced out of the passenger window. "I want to be alone."

The accident had zero effect on her stubbornness, as predicted. "You don't need to tackle this by yourself. She wants to be there for you and so do I. I hope you'll let us." He merged onto the highway and spared a glimpse at her. She leaned her head back on the headrest, closing her eyes. He returned his attention to the road. "Do you feel sick? Should I pull over?" The doctor mentioned her medication could cause dizziness.

"I'm fine. Keep going. I just want to get home."

And he wanted to be home with her. To go through the heartache and agony of losing Noah and Tracy, the first time must have been gut-wrenching. The idea that she had to endure the pain again, on her own, without understanding why she didn't have her husband to lean on—it crushed his heart.

No more words were spoken the entire hour back to Marlene's house. Brady helped her out of the truck and grabbed the small plastic bag of her belongings from the hospital. She stepped in and absorbed her surroundings while Brady followed behind and closed the door.

"Thanks, Brady, for everything. I guess you can go now," she said, her voice quiet. "I don't want to keep you."

"Are you sure? Do you need anything before I go?"

Or a lot of things, so he had a reason to stay?

She hobbled over to a table in the corner of the living room. Framed pictures covered almost every inch. Her fingers grazed over a white wooden frame with a distressed look. Her chin trembled as she picked up the picture.

Brady crossed the room without hesitation. He took the photo out of her hands. Marlene stood in the center, one arm around Noah and the other around Tracy. Noah wore a tux, Tracy a wedding gown, and Marlene a flowy green dress. Wide smiles stretched on their faces. Faith sat in front of them. Everyone looked so happy, and none of them had the faintest clue that Noah and Tracy would be gone a few days later.

A heavy weight pressed on his chest, as he set down the picture. This had been his family once, too. He hadn't been there to share this perfect moment with them, and he hadn't been there to hold Marlene up when it fell apart.

Marlene remained still, leaning on her crutches. He reached up and pushed a strand of hair behind her ear. When she didn't flinch, he wrapped his arms around her.

"I'm so sorry, Marlene." His voice trembled and he swallowed hard.

Something seemed to break inside her, and she let loose a deep, heartrending cry. "Why?" she asked between sobs. "How could this be real?" The pain in her voice tore him apart.

He stroked the back of her hair. "I wish I could take it away."

"I lost them and I lost you. Everything that matters is gone, and I don't even know why."

He hugged a little tighter, taking care not to throw her off balance. She dropped the crutches and clung to him, his heart breaking even more. "You didn't lose me, Marlene. I'm here."

Chapter Nine

Marlene did the one thing she swore she wouldn't. She bawled in Brady's arms. While she expected to go home to an empty house, she hadn't accounted for a table filled with happy memories, of which she had no recollection.

Noah and Tracy were the most beautiful bride and groom. Their wedding picture shredded her from the inside out.

"Why don't we sit down?" Brady said.

She nodded. He released her and leaned down to grab the crutches. She took them from him and hopped to the nearest chair, setting herself down. "I didn't mean to lose it like that—"

"Do not finish that sentence," Brady ordered. "You're more than allowed to be confused, angry, sad, you name it. This would be impossible for anyone to bear once, let alone a second time. Let it out, Marlene. Stop being so damn strong all the time, and just be."

She blew out a deep breath. "I'm fine now. I'm sure you have things to do. You can go. Thanks again for all your help."

A muscle ticked along his jaw. "You don't need to thank me, and I don't have anything to do. If you want me to go, I respect that, but if you don't, I'm happy to stay the night and sleep on the couch."

The last thing she wanted was for him to leave, but she needed to process her new surroundings. What if she leaned on him to get through this darkness, and then couldn't let him go? She didn't even know if he'd moved on. Her heart squeezed. What if he had a girl-friend?

She met his gaze. The love and compassion that seemed to shine in his deep blue eyes made what she was about to say even harder. "I think you should go."

His shoulders sagged. "I understand. I'll call you tomorrow, okay?"

"Sure." She forced a small smile.

Brady pressed his lips to her forehead. "I'll be as close or as far as you need me to be." He stood and walked out the front door.

Loneliness kicked in as Brady's truck roared to life and grew distant. The emptiness of the three-bedroom colonial she had inherited from her parents consumed her. This was her life now.

No Mom or Dad. No Noah. Not even Tracy, who she considered a little sister. And no Brady.

None of it made sense.

A fresh wave of hot tears streamed down her face. She hugged herself and let them come.

Marlene sat up on the living room couch and rubbed her eyes. Sun-shine spilled in through the picture window. Icicles hung off the edge of the roof, glistening and dripping.

Getting upstairs to the bedroom last night had been quite the pro-duction, but when she got there, she couldn't bring herself to sleep in the giant king-sized bed alone. She didn't dare enter any other rooms either, not being up for any additional surprises for the evening.

Someone rang the doorbell. "One second," Marlene called out, grabbing her crutches. Her leg throbbed as she rose from a seated position. She swung the door open and Ellen came in with Faith on a short leash. "Hey, Ellen. Thank you so much for taking care of her."

Ellen stepped inside and gave Marlene a one-handed hug, the other one keeping Faith from jumping all over them. "She's no problem. The kids loved sleeping with her. How are you feeling?"

Marlene tipped her head back, and then straightened. "The truth? Physically sore. Mentally confused."

She had been neighbors with Ellen for many years. The last Marlene recalled, they had been close friends, and it appeared they still were. Finally, a semblance of positive news she could appreciate.

The poor dog barked and cried, lunging for Marlene but unable to make contact. She reached out to pet Faith, trying to calm her. "I'm okay, girl," Marlene said.

Faith stopped yanking now that she was closer.

"Now Faith. Be gentle." Ellen unleashed Faith and she settled beside Marlene's feet. "Come on. I'm making breakfast." Ellen held up a small grocery bag Marlene hadn't noticed she was holding.

"You don't need to do that."

Ellen sighed. "I spend the majority of my time taking care of four hyperactive boys. Don't rob me of my girl time."

Marlene's eyebrows furrowed. "When did you have another baby?" Ellen had three beautiful sons the last Marlene checked. It was possible she could've had a fourth in the time Marlene lost. She frowned.

Ellen slipped off her shoes and padded toward the stove. "You're forgetting the original child of mine, Justin."

Relief washed over Marlene and she laughed. Justin, Ellen's husband, was a giant kid, but in the best way possible.

"Take a seat. Talk to me." Ellen emptied the bag, revealing bacon and eggs. She made her way around the kitchen as if it were her own, pulling out frying pans and utensils, and getting a pot of coffee going.

"So, how much do you know about what happened?" Marlene asked.

"Brady told me about the broken leg and the memory loss. I can't lie. I'm burning with questions and concerns about what you don't remember, but I don't want to overwhelm you."

The heaviness in Marlene's chest lightened ever so slightly. Ellen possessed the rare ability to offer support without being invasive, never pushing for information. It had always been her superpower.

"It seems I picked a terrible time to forget." Marlene's eyes stung.

The smell of bacon filled the room. Ellen stood at the stove with a spatula in hand, shaking her head. "Or the best, depending on how you look at it." She placed the food on two plates and carried them over to the table. Turning back around, she fixed coffee for each of them and then sat across from Marlene. "Are you holding up okay?"

Marlene bit the inside of her lip. "I haven't wrapped my head around everything yet." She played with the handle of her mug. "But my heart hurts."

Wetness pooled in Ellen's eyes. "I'm sorry, Marlene. We've talked about all of it before so I could try to help you remember, but only if that's what you want."

Marlene swallowed hard. "Thanks, but I'm not ready." She scooped up a forkful of eggs and shoved it in her mouth. She couldn't think about what happened to her and Brady or Noah and Tracy without being a blubbery mess. The little voice in her head told her to wait until her emotions were in check. Maybe Ellen could help with one thing she didn't understand that didn't fill her with grief though. "Did

I explain why I would leave my job in Mistport to commute an hour away? What the hell was I thinking?"

Ellen set her fork down. "Small town life was getting on your last nerve. People feel awful about everything that's been thrown at you, and for some bizarre reason, you take that as a bad thing. We disagree on this point, in case you can't tell."

"I wouldn't want everyone's pity."

Ellen smirked. "Are you sure you lost your memory? I'm pretty sure we've had this conversation already." She threaded her fingers together and studied her palms before flicking her gaze up to Marlene's. "What you just said, that's exactly why you did it. You were even talking about selling this house."

"What?" Marlene squeaked. "I would never." That was news Brady didn't relay, but then again, if they were divorced, he probably didn't know.

Ellen shrugged. "I prayed you wouldn't, but I haven't faced the things you've been through. You're supposed to stay here and be my neighbor forever." She flashed a sad smile.

"I guess I should call my job and let them know I'll be out for a while." Marlene had no idea what her boss's name was.

"No need. Brady and I picked up your car yesterday and he talked to the woman who called him from the hospital and your boss. They're going to check on you in a few days, but they said you can call them if you're up to it." Ellen reached into her pocket for her phone and poked at the screen. "I texted you their information."

Marlene's life resembled nothing like a younger version of herself would have imagined. She stared down at her empty plate. "Thanks. And thank you for breakfast, too."

"It was nothing. I'm so glad you're home." Ellen cleared the table and stuck the dishes in the dishwasher. "I've got to go. The cable guy is coming and my window is ten a.m. until the end of time. Wouldn't want to miss him."

Marlene chuckled.

"I'm only a phone call away. Holler if you need help with Faith or want to talk about anything."

Marlene nodded. "I will." She hobbled to the door with Ellen.

Ellen slipped on her shoes. She grasped the doorknob and peered over her shoulder.

"What is it?" Marlene asked. Memory gone or not, she sensed hesitation.

Ellen's lips went thin. "Be careful with Brady. He wrecked you when you guys started crumbling." She turned to give Marlene a quick hug. "I don't want you to get hurt."

Chapter Ten

B rady glanced at the online menu for *Sid's Pizza*. He called in an order for pick-up.

"What'cha doin?" Scott asked in a high-pitched, girly voice as he hovered above Brady's shoulder.

Brady jumped.

"You didn't ask for your usual." Scott stepped back and crossed his arms.

"So?" Brady asked.

"I happen to know one person that's adamant about their extra cheese pizza from Sid's."

Brady rolled his eyes. "Do you have a point?"

Scott landed a soft punch on Brady's arm. "No, little brother. I'm glad you're listening to me for once. Go get her." He grabbed his coat. "I'm heading home."

"Bye," Brady said as Scott walked out.

An hour later, he found himself ringing Marlene's doorbell. He should've texted or called, but he didn't want to give her a chance to say no. She still might send him away, but it would be harder for her to do face-to-face.

It was weird to stand on the front stoop of a house he had lived in for years and wait to be invited in, not that he could blame anyone but himself. How did he miss the signs that she was getting sick of him leaving?

Marlene opened the door, her mouth falling open.

"I thought you might be hungry." Brady held up the pizza box.

Her gaze searched his. If only he understood what she was looking for.

"Oh, you didn't have to," Marlene said, running a finger along the handle of one crutch.

"I wanted to," Brady said.

She stepped backward. "Come in."

Brady headed for the kitchen and made quick work of grabbing plates and pouring two glasses of water. He motioned for her to sit and set a slice of the pie on each plate. "How are you today?"

"Same as yesterday. My leg still hurts if I stay in one position too long."

Dark circles lined Marlene's hazel eyes. She rubbed the heel of her palm against her chest in an almost absent-minded kind of way. "How'd you sleep?"

"Not well."

He waited for her to say more, but she took a bite of pizza instead. Whenever he tried to draw the hard truth out of her, she always made him work for it. Tonight would be no different.

"Were you uncomfortable?" he asked.

"Partly."

He wanted to yank the hair out of his head. "And the other part?"

She finished chewing and took a sip of her drink. "I don't want to talk about it."

This was the moment where their conversation typically blew up into a full-blown fight. She would tell him to quit interrogating her, while he would plead with her to stop pushing him away. He resisted the urge to press for an answer.

"Okay," he said, gritting his teeth.

Marlene's brows knitted together as they finished off dinner. Brady held back all the questions brewing in his mind.

They both got up and cleared the table. He offered to take care of the mess himself, but she wouldn't listen. Typical Marlene.

"Why are you really here?" She opened the dishwasher and placed the glasses and plates inside.

He took a deep breath, then exhaled. "I'm worried about you."

If his honesty pissed her off, well, too bad. He would support her through this train wreck of a situation, as long as she'd let him. No matter how much she had come to hate him, the feeling was never mutual.

He waited for a sign of anger or frustration from her, but it never came. A blank expression remained on her face. "What happened to us?" she asked, her voice cracking.

Heaviness settled in his chest. At least she wanted to know. "We should probably sit down. It's not a short story."

They migrated to the living room. He froze as he took in the pillows on the couch and the rumpled blankets in a pile. "Did you sleep here last night?"

Marlene leaned on both crutches and picked up the bedding, tossing it on the nearby chair. "Yeah."

Brady stifled a groan. Her one-word answers weren't new, and they never ceased to bug the hell out of him.

She sunk back into the cushions and closed her eyes. "I couldn't bring myself to stay in my room. Didn't feel right."

He fought the itch to ask her why because doing so would clam her up.

At least the nugget of information she offered brought him a glimmer of hope. The bed she couldn't lay in had once been theirs, and even though he didn't want her in anguish, her reaction meant they had a fighting chance.

"What's wrong with the guest room?" he asked, trying not to focus the conversation on their relationship. He settled on the opposite end of the sofa.

She shrugged. "I wasn't sure if it still was a guest room and I didn't have the strength to find out. There are things all around me that give clues about what I don't remember, but it's like navigating through a mine field. Random, seemingly mundane things set me off in an emotional spiral. Between that and the physical hurt, I just can't—" She dropped her head in her hands.

He moved to her side before he could overthink his actions. He draped an arm around her shoulders and pulled her in.

"So, the couch works for now. No more surprises in here." She kept her face covered.

Marlene had been surprised last night, and not in a good way, either. He imagined her trudging through the house and finding countless other memories that had the same effect. Brady rubbed her arm lightly. "It's killing me that you're dealing with this alone."

"Don't pity me, please," she said.

"That's not it," he said. "I messed up by not fighting to keep us together, by not seeing your point of view and not trying to change. I regretted it from the moment we separated. Then when Noah and Tracy died, I wanted to be there for you, but you pushed me away." His hand cupped her cheek, tilting her head so he could meet her gaze. "I've never stopped loving you."

"Are you saying I asked for the divorce?" Marlene asked.

He nodded. "I could sense your irritation whenever I left you, but I had no gauge on how fed up you were with it. I was convinced you'd come with me eventually. I was blind."

She frowned. "I couldn't leave Noah. He wasn't a kid anymore, but he wasn't exactly an adult."

He took a deep breath. If he wanted a real shot with her, he had to be honest. It would do him no good if she woke up tomorrow with all her memories intact and he had lied about any of it. He wasn't going to screw this up.

"You remember how I usually came back for a few months between assignments?"

Marlene nodded into his chest.

"When I was in Prague, I lined up my next stint in Italy, so I would only be home for a week before taking off again. I begged you to join me. The place was on our bucket list so it seemed perfect to me, but you dished out an ultimatum instead. Break the contract or break our marriage."

She pulled away enough to look up at him. "And you just left?" A hurt expression filled her shiny eyes.

"I'm sorry." His throat thickened. "I wish I chose differently."

She broke from his hold and leaned back against the couch. "I don't know if I can do this alone."

"Then don't." His chest ached. She was the strongest person he ever met. For her to admit fear made it almost impossible for him to breathe.

"We've been running into each other at Murray's a lot since you started your new job. I was working up the nerve to ask you on a date." He turned to her. "I'm not going to push you, but you seem confused about my actions. I thought if I told you where I was coming from, it'd make more sense."

She leaned on his shoulder and slipped her arm through his. They remained that way in the quiet. Marlene was never one of those women who liked having heart-to-heart conversations. This single gesture suggested she would consider what he said, and that was more than he could hope for at the moment. He glanced down at her drooping eyes.

"Marlene, you need a proper night's rest." He squeezed her hand. "Come on. I'll help you upstairs."

"I can't," she replied.

He couldn't leave her camped out on the couch. "Why don't I check the guest room? I'll shove anything I don't recognize into the closet, and then you can settle in." He bolted out of the living room and up the stairs before she protested.

Brady cracked open the door and breathed a sigh of relief. The curtains and the bedding were as he remembered. No visible pictures of friends or family adorned the walls. A black and white poster of a huge oak tree still hung above the headboard. A pile of empty boxes sat in the corner, but other than that, nothing alarming hid in plain sight.

He made his way back to Marlene. "It's all set for you up there."

Her brows creased. "Okay." She stood and grabbed her crutches, a perplexed expression on her face.

When they got into the room, Brady pulled back the covers. Marlene lingered beyond the doorway.

"Are you alright?" he asked.

"Yeah. I should grab pajamas."

"Take a seat." He patted the bed. "If everything is still in the same place, I'll bring it to you, if that doesn't bother you."

"You don't have to," she said.

"Marlene, I know I don't. Stop putting up a fight."

She exhaled and lowered herself on to the mattress. "Thanks."

He ran over to their old room and ignored the nostalgic pang in his chest. He grabbed flannel pajama pants and an oversized t-shirt, then headed into the master bathroom and snatched her toothbrush and toothpaste.

He returned to Marlene and placed everything in her hands. "I'm going to let you rest now. Can I come back tomorrow and check on you?"

She glanced up at him, seeming to be searching his face again like she did earlier. "Would you stay with me instead?"

Chapter Eleven

M arlene covered her mouth. The words escaped before she thought them through, and she wanted to crawl into a deep dark hole and never climb out. "Pretend I never said that."

Brady kneeled in front of her and pushed her hair behind her ear. "I would love to stay."

His voice was sweet and tender, and it melted Marlene into a puddle of goo. She needed him. If she woke up tomorrow and remembered why she was supposed to hate him, she would deal with it then. For the moment, the only person who could help her weather this storm was Brady.

He rose to his feet and pulled her up. She headed for the bathroom to change and do her nightly routine. When she returned, he peeled back the covers and stacked up pillows at the end of the bed. She lay back while he helped her position her leg on its perch. Relief surged through her as the blood rushed away from her throbbing foot.

Brady draped the blankets over her. "I'll be downstairs. Yell if you need anything." He turned away.

"Brady?" His presence calmed her. The idea of him not being with her didn't.

"Yes?" he asked.

"Would you...stay here with me?" She bit her bottom lip. Was this too much?

"Are you sure?" he asked. "We should take things slow."

Marlene looked into his eyes. "I don't want to sleep alone."

"Okay. I'll be right back." He disappeared and then came back a minute later. He kicked off his shoes and slid beneath the covers fully dressed, before turning off the bedside lamp.

Was she making a huge mistake?

All her life, she had been strong. She always stood her ground and dealt with the hardest things with no one to depend on but herself. For one night, she would let her pride go and let someone take care of her for a change.

"Brady?" she whispered.

"Hmm?" he asked.

"I feel broken." She reached for his hand and laced her fingers in his. "Every time I think of Noah and Tracy, I can barely breathe." There was something about being with him in the dark. The darkness gave her courage to speak.

"You'll get through this."

With him by her side, maybe she could.

"Would you hold me?" She had to be vocal about what she needed, and she hurt enough to not care about weakness. He said he wasn't going to push, and the man always kept his word.

The weight on the bed shifted and Brady settled close to her, on her uninjured side. He rested his head on her pillow and slung his arm over her body, resting his hand on her waist.

"Are you comfortable?" he asked.

"Yes." Warmth bloomed in her chest and spread to her limbs as his breath tickled her ear.

He kissed her on the cheek. "Sweet dreams, Marlene."

"Good night."

Eventually, Brady's breathing pattern changed, and he fell fast asleep. Marlene lay awake, soaking in his closeness, praying for the night to pass slowly. She wanted to stay entangled with him as long as possible.

Chapter Twelve

B rady woke to a buzzing in his pocket. He removed his arm from Marlene's side and yanked out his phone. Scott was calling, but Scott could wait. He pressed *Ignore*.

"Who is it?" Marlene asked in a scratchy voice.

"Just Scott. I'll talk to him later." He could survive without Brady's free labor for one day. Even though they had their fair share of disagreements, his brother would understand his absence in this case.

"You should call him back. He might be worried about you not coming home." Marlene rubbed her eyes.

Brady let out a soft laugh. "I'm a grown man, Marlene. He probably wants to know if I'm going to work. I'm still helping him while Trina's on bed rest."

Concern flickered in her eyes. As though Marlene didn't have enough on her mind, she still cared about how everyone else was doing. Her heart seemed to have no bounds. "Is she okay?"

"Yeah. She's great." Brady rolled up on his side and balanced on his elbow. "She's following the doctor's orders to take it easy but she says she feels fine. I offered to pitch in until the fall. Scott runs a successful business, but he can't do the paperwork to save his life."

Marlene placed a hand on her chest. "Wow." Her lips curved upward. Brady vowed to make that happen more often.

"Yeah. Can you believe it?"

"Trina always wanted a baby, and now she'll have three. I'm really happy for them."

It had taken Scott a while to warm up to the idea of kids, but once Trina convinced him they should go for it, he jumped right in. He doted on Trina, catering to her every need.

Not that Brady blamed him. If Marlene was carrying his kid, he would—

Wait. Did he really allow that thought into his head?

"Brady?" Marlene asked, shaking him out of his thoughts.

"Sorry, what?"

"I was saying you should help him. I'll be okay."

He glanced over at her. Would she let him come back later? How much was too much? For so long, he had wanted another chance with her. He needed to find a way to show her without going overboard.

"I like taking care of you." The words sounded corny to his own ears, but they were true.

"That's sweet, but I can manage," she said.

He had promised not to push. Refusing to leave her house after she politely hinted at it probably fell into the pushy category. He sighed, not wanting to get out of bed. "Fine. Will you call or text me if you need anything?" he asked.

"Yeah, of course," she answered.

Fat chance in hell of that happening. She never asked for help ever. The frown formed on his face, as if he had no control over it.

"But, if I don't, would you come back tonight anyway?" She stared down at the sheets.

Heat radiated in his chest. "On one condition."

She raised an eyebrow. "Which is?"

"Let me make you dinner."

She tilted her head. "You learned how to cook?"

"Nope," Brady said, earning a confused laugh from her. The sound soothed his insides, filling the holes in his heart that ached for her happiness. He hoped to make that a common occurrence.

"I don't understand," she said.

"Come on. I can make a few things. Give me some credit." He tickled her side without thinking, something he used to do all the time. She bubbled with laughter. "Don't you remember my specialty? It's the right day and everything."

Recognition dawned on her face. "Taco Tuesday. We're having tacos." She smiled.

"Yup." He still didn't want to move, but he didn't want to overstay his welcome. Their evening plans made it a little easier. "I'll see you later, then?"

She nodded.

What was life without taking a chance? He leaned over and kissed her on the cheek.

Chapter Thirteen

M arlene stared at the ceiling of the guest bedroom. Was she making a mistake, pushing for Brady to re-enter her life? It was hard to judge when she couldn't recall why they got divorced in the first place.

She closed her eyes and tried to remember. Yes, she hated his prolonged absences, but never had the big 'D' word entered the picture. No clues emerged from the depths of her mind. Screw it. She loved him, and he seemed to still love her. A second chance seemed a better alternative than resisting the urge to be with someone who shared mutual feelings. For once, she would follow her heart.

Well, that settled one topic, and now for the next. What about work? She left a wonderful job five minutes from her house and took one far away. Why would she do such a thing and did she want to continue with it?

A whiny sound came from the side of the bed. Marlene glanced over the edge and discovered Faith laying on the carpet, her tail swooshing back and forth in slow motion.

"Hey, there's my sweet girl." Faith came over and licked Marlene's hand. Luckily, Noah had trained Faith to let herself in and out of the house using a doggy door he installed in his basement apartment. It would come in handy while Marlene recovered, leaving her only to worry about making sure the dog ate twice a day.

At least Noah left her with a loyal companion. Her breath caught in her throat. How could he be gone?

She lifted her leg off the heap of pillows and sat upright. The question bounced around in her head as she stood, retrieved a fresh set of clothes from her bedroom, and headed for the bathroom. She freed a garbage bag from the pile she had stashed beneath the sink and stripped down. After carefully wrapping her cast, she turned on the water and lowered herself onto the built-in shower bench, pointing the protected leg away from the stream that rained down.

The warm spray soothed her nerves. She lathered up and considered how to spend the day. Her pain level seemed much more manageable, and she couldn't bear the idea of moping around the house. Instead of beating herself up to remember the past, she would get a handle on the present.

Marlene wasn't the kind of girl who took a long time to get ready in the morning, but a broken limb slowed her down considerably. After what seemed an eternity, she sat at the kitchen table with Faith at her feet and pulled up the contact information for the boss she didn't remember, Carlos. She took a deep breath. Calling this stranger and asking about her job made her stomach churn, so she took the wimpy way out. She started to text.

Marlene: "Hi. I was wondering if I could stop by today to talk to you. I have a lot of questions."

She rolled her eyes at herself. Wasn't that the truth?

Carlos: "So glad to hear from you. We're all thinking of you and hoping for a speedy recovery. If you're up to it, how about 3 p.m.?"

In addition to her curiosity, heading in to the office might trigger her memory. She had been pushing off the neurologist appointment, trying to handle the situation on her own. They wouldn't be able to fix her, so what would be the point?

Marlene checked the railway schedule. With her right leg out of commission, she would be unable to drive. She confirmed the time with Carlos and texted Ellen next.

Marlene: "I need a ride to the train station around noon. Would you mind dropping me off?"

Ellen: "No problem. I was going to check on you anyway. See you then."

Marlene: "You're the best. Thank you."

She put the phone down and exhaled. At least her relationship with Ellen was as she remembered it. Marlene filled with gratitude.

A few hours later, Marlene sat in the minivan, struggling to understand the tight set of Ellen's jaw as she talked about Brady spending the night.

"I wasn't expecting you to be upset." Marlene's brows furrowed.

Ellen stopped at an intersection and glanced over at Marlene, her lips pressed together with a faint grimace. "That's not the right word."

"What is, then?" Marlene asked.

The light turned green. Ellen turned her attention back to the road. "I don't know. Concerned, maybe? Letting him go wasn't easy. I'm afraid he'll hurt you again, and I can't watch it a second time."

Ellen pulled up to the passenger drop-off area.

"I appreciate that you're worried, but Brady isn't pushing me. I think it's more me than him. He told me about how things ended."

"Did he now?" Ellen asked, a hint of skepticism in her voice. "We should compare notes on that."

In her heart, Marlene believed Ellen was her closest friend and wanted her to be happy. Ellen's mistrust of Brady freaked her out. A discussion wasn't a terrible idea.

"Okay, but I can't miss this train. How about tomorrow? Coffee?" She leaned in to give Ellen a hug.

"Yes, definitely. Text me if you need a ride home."

"Thank you." Marlene climbed out of the car and settled on her crutches. She shut the door and headed for the platform.

An hour later, she stood in front of a building that she would swear she had never seen before in her life. The security guard greeted her by name and asked how she was doing. She politely answered his questions, not wanting to tell him she had no clue who he was.

She wished the man well, as she stepped into the elevator and pressed the button for the fifth floor. When the doors parted, she approached the receptionist desk where a cluster of women chatted among themselves.

One of them was a tall, attractive blonde who appeared to be in her mid-twenties. She struck Marlene as familiar, but she couldn't put her finger on why. Another seemed to be around Marlene's height with gorgeous, wavy red hair. The third woman sat behind the desk. She was petite, with porcelain skin, jet-black hair, and red-rimmed glasses.

"Marlene!" the redhead called, waving her arms in enthusiastic greeting. "I'm so happy to see you." Like the man in the lobby, Marlene had no recollection of the friendly woman. Were they friends? What was the proper etiquette to re-meet people who obviously knew her?

The other two women remained quiet and flashed tentative smiles.

"Um, hi." Marlene leaned on her uninjured side and gripped the handle tighter. "I'm meeting with Carlos at three. I'm sorry. Do we work together?"

The excited redhead dropped her gaze to the floor, seeming to deflate before Marlene's eyes. A knot formed in Marlene's stomach.

The blonde woman stepped forward. "We do. I'm Paige, and this is Sierra." She gestured toward the dejected woman. "And this is Sandy, our receptionist." Sandy waved.

"Did we meet at the hospital?" Marlene asked.

Paige nodded. "Yes, that was me." She clasped her hands together in front of her. "I owe you a massive apology. What's happening to you is my fault."

"No, it's not." Paige had to be the co-worker Marlene pushed out of the way. She had no reason to feel bad about Marlene's decision to shove her to safety.

"Why don't we walk you to Carlos's office?" Paige lifted her arm, motioning down the long hall. "He's wrapping up a call with our biggest client in San Diego. It's one of your accounts, actually."

Marlene followed Sierra's lead with Paige walking beside her. "So I support companies on the west coast?"

Sierra glanced over her shoulder at Paige, a strained expression on her face. "Yes. All three of us do. We're a team."

Paige's chin dipped. What weren't they telling her? They arrived at Carlos's door and knocked. "Come in," a man's voice called out.

"We'll talk to you soon," Paige said.

"We're going to help you get on track when you come back to work," Sierra added.

"That would be incredible. Thank you," Marlene said. The pair turned and walked away. She took a deep breath and opened the door. The man sitting behind the desk wore a warm smile.

"Marlene, I was relieved to hear from you. Take a seat, please."

She settled into a chair across from him. "Paige filled me in on what happened and I also spoke with your significant other." Marlene nodded, noticing he didn't call Brady her husband. It made her uneasy, but it wasn't this man's fault. Brady wasn't. "You know what? Hang on one second." Carlos stood, closed the door and promptly returned to his seat.

Marlene rubbed her clammy hands on her lap. "Are you going to fire me?"

Carlos's eyes widened. "No, I didn't want other people to overhear our conversation. I'm sorry if I worried you."

"It's okay." Marlene sighed. "I'm going to be honest with you. I don't remember anything about this place."

Carlos nodded. "I know. Why don't we discuss your job, and then we can decide where to go from there. No pressure. Let's just talk."

He flashed a reassuring smile. The man seemed to be genuinely concerned.

"Okay," she said.

"You're part of the sales and client support team for the west coast region. Sierra and Paige, who I believe you've already seen today, are your teammates. As far as I can tell, the three of you have become fast friends."

Marlene agreed with the assessment. "It's nice to have friends at work." At her old job, the one she doesn't remember leaving, she adored her co-workers.

"It is, and, especially in this case."

Marlene's eyebrows wrinkled. "Why is that?"

"Because you're scheduled to move to our new San Diego office with them in the spring."

Marlene could feel her mouth gaping, but she couldn't seem to close it. "I'm sorry. What?"

Carlos splayed his hand across the desk and rubbed his thumb along the surface. "I don't know the specifics of your personal plans, but your first working day out there is May fifteenth."

Her stomach clenched. "That's soon."

"Yes. I realize this is a lot to process, so I'm going to level with you," Carlos said. "You picked up your responsibilities quickly when you started and I'm confident you can do it again. When I asked you what attracted you to the position, the opportunity to relocate sat at the top of the list."

"Oh." Marlene strained to dig into the depths of her mind to figure out what was happening. Nothing emerged.

"Marlene, I can tell you're surprised, and I have a suggestion. Give yourself a few days to think this through and we'll talk again on Monday. Does that sound fair?"

She nodded as her chest constricted.

"Good. I hope to keep you on board, Marlene. You're an excellent employee. So, I'll see you again soon?"

Marlene stood. "Yes."

Less than a week to determine her future, with a gaping hole in her recent past? She reminded herself, it could always be worse.

Chapter Fourteen

Marlene exited the office building and caught the shuttle bus that would take her to the train station. Her arrival time was perfect, with only minutes to spare before the next departure. She hobbled to the nearest car and settled at a window seat.

She stared out the glass as they pulled away from the platform. Her pre-accident plans turned her life on its head. The decision to leave couldn't have come easy, and yet, she had made it.

Her gut reaction to quit gave her pause. Any minute now she could remember everything. There was a possibility she would kick herself for letting the opportunity go.

Why would she ever consider anywhere but Mistport home? Her throat tightened. At the ripe old age of thirty-one she had experienced tremendous changes, any one of which were difficult to absorb, let alone jumbled together.

Her parents had died when she was eighteen, struck by a drunk driver in broad daylight on a beautiful, bright sunny day. She would never forget when the policeman knocked on the front door and delivered the news. The carefree college student in her disintegrated as the man apologized, left the house, and drove off in his police cruiser.

Next came the divorce, she didn't remember, to a man she couldn't imagine being without. According to Brady, he hadn't seen it coming.

She didn't fit the stereotype of the woman who talked things through and worked out problems. For better or worse, she accepted this as one of her flaws. Sharing her feelings and the like made her want to hurl. Not for this girl. No thank you.

Then the unthinkable happened, Noah and Tracy's tragic car accident. Of all the things she couldn't recall, this seemed, by far, the most significant and the least believable. The hollow ache in her chest expanded, paralyzing her with a grief that went bone deep.

Any of these events warranted a fresh start.

When she arrived at the station, she headed for the taxi stand and climbed in a cab. Brady or Ellen would've picked her up, but she couldn't face either of them yet. Moving to California meant leaving them behind and she couldn't explain why she would've wanted it. She prayed for all the reasons hidden deep in the recesses of her mind to come back to her.

An older man with silver hair peered at her through the rear-view mirror. "Hi, Miss. What's the address?"

"151 Breezy Point Lane, please." She set the crutches beside her and shut the door.

The man hit the button to get the meter running and started to drive. As the car turned onto the main road, Marlene's phone vibrated. She discovered an email notification from a man she didn't recognize.

Marlene,

The paperwork is still being drafted, but the Clarks agreed to the ninety-day closing you requested. They accepted your terms to purchase as-is, regardless of the pending inspection they scheduled. Call with any questions. Otherwise, I'll be in touch soon.

Regards, Matt

Matthew Moore

Moore Realty Group, Inc.

Marlene's heart dropped to her feet. She sold the house? Even if she decided to stay, where would she live? What the hell had she been thinking just days ago? She slipped the phone back in her coat pocket and hugged herself in her seat.

Marlene paid the driver when he stopped in her driveway and walked into the house. Faith ran up to her and jumped around, tail wagging so hard her butt wagged, too.

"Hi Faithy. I missed you, too." Marlene pet the happy dog, grateful to have a companion that didn't want anything except love. Faith disappeared and tore through the house, running laps around the kitchen and living room. She celebrated Marlene's arrival as if she had been gone for weeks, rather than a few hours. Marlene laughed.

Later that evening, Brady knocked on her door with a bunch of grocery bags in his hand. His face lit up when she let him in. A knot formed in her stomach. After much deliberation, she concluded she wouldn't tell Brady and Ellen about her plans immediately. Neither of them mentioned her moving, so she ventured a guess that they weren't aware.

No need to worry them if it might not even happen.

"Are you ready for a fancy meal?" A wave of heat swept through her as he stepped into her personal space and dragged a light finger down her arm. One side of his mouth kicked up.

"Gourmet tacos?" she asked, holding back a laugh as her pulse quickened.

"That's right." He headed for the kitchen.

They unloaded the contents of the bags on the counter. Brady pulled out a pan and began frying the meat for their meal while Marlene propped herself on her crutches and chopped tomatoes.

Brady whistled one of his favorite songs, *Patience* by Guns N' Roses. A light, fluttery feeling stirred in her chest, the first sign of contentment to pass through her since she woke in the hospital. Standing with him in comfortable silence was the only place she wanted to be.

Strange whispers teetered at the edge of her mind.

Choose. Me or your wanderlust. You can't have both. Not anymore.

Was this the ultimatum Brady mentioned last night? She shook her head. Anger accompanied those words. Marlene recognized the sentiment in a detached way, as if she were observing someone else's emotions.

"What's up?" Brady dipped his chin to meet her gaze. Marlene had been so engrossed in her possible memory relapse, she missed that he had finished cooking. He stood beside her holding a tray with taco fixings. An empty bowl sat on the platter, presumably for the tomatoes sitting in front of her.

"Oh, nothing. Sorry." She filled the dish and set it back in place.

He stepped back and gave a hesitating nod. She sucked at lying, especially to him. She turned away and headed for the table, biting her bottom lip.

"How was your day?" Brady asked.

"Eventful." Marlene sprinkled shredded cheese on a taco she constructed. "I got restless after you left, so I decided to call my boss to find out more about my new job."

His eyebrows lifted. "How'd it go?"

She glanced down at her plate before looking back at him. "Okay. I, uh, actually met with him in person."

"I hope you didn't drive." Brady's over-protectiveness kicked in. A perplexed expression crossed his face.

"No. Ellen dropped me at the train station. There's a shuttle bus that runs from the station to the office. It was an easy trip."

"Wow. That is...eventful. It went well?" Brady bit into his taco with a loud crunch. Marlene sensed the wheels turning in his mind.

"It did. I'm going back to work next week." And making a major life decision before then. Minor detail.

Brady finished chewing, then swallowed. "So soon? You'll be ready?"

She shrugged. "I don't see what hanging around the house will do for me. Maybe getting back to my routine will help with my memory and all."

"Good point." His words were positive, but a pained expression passed over him. He replaced it with a smile, but the corners of his eyes didn't squint together like they usually did when he was happy. He put down the taco. "Can I ask you something?"

This was one of Brady's favorite phrases, constantly asking permission to ask a question. She let out a short laugh, since she never refused. "Yes. Just ask, Brady."

"If you remember something about me, and it either upsets you or angers you, will you talk to me about it?"

She met his gaze. Intensity shone there. She turned away. "I don't know."

And that was the truth. Opening up wasn't natural to her. Depending on how traumatic the memory would be, she couldn't guarantee she would be able to say anything at all.

"I hope you will." He sucked in a breath deep enough to raise his broad shoulders. "I messed up everything with you. No matter what happens, I'm sorry, and I love you."

Her chest tightened. She loved him, too. So much.

A wave of frustration rolled through her. They loved each other, yet they were divorced, and she was scheduled to move to the opposite end of the country in the spring.

Why the hell would she do that? The doctor warned she may never remember. She might not ever understand why she craved such a drastic change. What she did know was that she wanted this man, and didn't want to let him go. She stood.

"What are you doing?" Brady asked.

She leaned on the tabletop and hopped over to him. He glanced around the room, his brows creased. She stopped in front of him, balancing on one foot. "Don't let me fall."

He tilted his head up toward her, seeming to get ready to ask a question. Marlene didn't give him a chance, holding the silence by pressing her lips firmly to his.

Chapter Fifteen

B rady rose to his feet and wrapped his arms around Marlene. Scorching heat rooted deep in his gut, spreading through him like wildfire. His senses became hyperaware of all things Marlene. The smell of her strawberry-scented perfume surrounded him, bringing him back to a time when they were happy, fueling him with hope that they could go back.

He tilted his head, sweeping his tongue across her lips. She opened for him, allowing him to deepen the kiss. Her body melded with his, and she let out a soft moan. Brady poured all his love for Marlene into this kiss, a silent promise that if she gave him one more chance, he would build a new life with her, one that resembled what both of them wanted.

Marlene's cell vibrated on the table, breaking the spell. She pulled away but didn't make a move for the phone. Her gaze locked on his, her expression unreadable. She reached up and grazed the back of her hand across his five o'clock shadow. Never big on words when her emotions overwhelmed her, she chose to say nothing. Brady wasn't surprised.

"I think you missed the call," Brady said. Way to go, Captain Obvious.

"If it's important, they'll leave a message." Breathiness coated her tone and her chest rose and fell. She seemed as shocked as him by her own actions.

Instead of asking a million questions about what this meant, Brady followed her lead. No pressure he had told her only two nights ago. She made the first move, and he was not upset in the least. He would go with it.

"Why don't we get you off your feet? If you're not too tired, we could watch a movie." It would give them a chance to be with each other and without the need to talk if Marlene didn't want to go there.

"Sounds great." She reached for her crutches.

"I'll clean up. Want to start the search?"

Marlene smirked. The two of them always struggled with finding movies they both enjoyed. "Does that mean I choose?"

Brady carried the dirty dishes over to the sink. "We'll see." He might consider giving in this time, if she promised there would be a next. He made quick work of getting the kitchen in order and joined Marlene in the living room. She had settled on the couch with her leg propped up on the ottoman, remote control in hand.

"So what did you find?" Brady sat on the opposite end, even though he wanted to be right next to her.

She bit her bottom lip. "I'm feeling a little nicer than usual this evening. I picked three movies. You make the final call." She inclined her head.

That was a first. She never let him decide, and she always chose something he hated. Whenever he would protest, she would remind him of the saying, *Happy wife, happy life*, and he conceded every time. Then again, he had no idea what the options were. They might all be terrible.

He raised an eyebrow. "What are the choices?"

"Well, of course one is a romance. I bet you won't choose that one even though it's probably amazing. The Best of Me, you know, the Nicholas Sparks movie."

Brady rolled his eyes. "Next."

"Fine." Marlene tossed a throw pillow at him. "You're so predictable. Behold option two, Pitch Perfect."

Brady tilted his head at the latest suggestion. "The musical?"

"So you haven't seen it?" she asked.

"Can't say it was on my list of must-see movies."

"I read a few reviews. People seem to think it's really funny."

He sighed. Marlene could use a laugh. "What's the last one?"

"A new Captain America movie I've never heard of. The Winter Soldier?"

Brady fought back the frown tugging on his lips. She had chewed him out about seeing it in the theater by herself. It was one of the many things she exploded about, an example of why being married to him was a lonely existence. He swallowed.

"I've seen that one. The first one's better." His opinion wasn't a lie. Not exactly. He rubbed the back of his neck. A ball of unease took up residence in the pit of his stomach. "Let's go with the funny one."

She leaned back into the cushions and turned toward him. "Really?"

He nodded.

She pressed two fingers to her parted lips as she made the selection on the controller. "I guess you're not so predictable after all. Or maybe you are."

His cheeks flushed. Did she remember? Was he the biggest idiot known to man for not admitting the significance of the movie?

"You don't want me drooling over Chris Evans. Admit it." A triumphant smile spread on her face and she patted the empty seat beside her. "Come on jealous guy, come sit over here."

Brady never cared about the celebrities Marlene gushed over. Her appreciation of another man's physical appearance didn't threaten him, but he had to seize the perfect out she provided. "Something like that." He joined her on the other side of the couch. She took his arm and slung it over her shoulder, nestling into his side. She softened against him, and he kissed the top of her head. "Are you sure you're okay with this?"

"Never been better."

Well, who was he to argue?

Chapter Sixteen

Marlene threw precaution out the window. With a possible move to California on the horizon, she had to figure out if she and Brady could start over. He stayed true to his promise, remaining respectful of her space, but accepting whatever she offered.

No matter what Ellen revealed about the rocky past, Marlene couldn't dwell on it. She had to look toward the future. Major changes could be around the corner, and fate didn't care if she had all the pieces put together or not.

Her thoughts wandered as her eyes remained fixed on the television. Lucky for her, it didn't take a lot of brain power to follow the plot. She could still laugh at the hilarious scenes while keeping the major issues she faced in the back of her mind.

When the credits rolled, Marlene turned off the TV.

"Are you tired?" Brady asked.

She yawned. "Yeah. Long day."

"You should get to bed." Brady stood and stretched out his hand, pulling Marlene to her feet.

"Will you stay with me again?" Marlene grabbed her crutches and met his gaze.

His forehead wrinkled. He cupped her cheek. "I would love to, but I'm a little worried. Aren't we moving too fast? I don't want you to regret anything."

She held the same concern, but she was working on an accelerated timeline. "You make me...not sad." As soon as the words left her mouth, she wanted to take them back. This was why she didn't do the talking thing. She sucked at it.

Brady leaned in and gave her a soft kiss on the lips. "What I'm really going for is happy, but I'll earn my way back to you. I promise."

She took a deep breath. "This is going to sound crazy, but I want to give us a chance now, in case I remember the bad times. I've experienced so much loss, so much sorrow, but all of it was due to unforeseen circumstances. What happened to my parents and Noah were beyond my control." She covered Brady's hand with her own. "You and me, us being together, we have a say, and I say we're worth it. I want to focus on what I can change, and accept what I can't. I love you, Brady, and I don't want to stop loving you. Not ever."

His eyes lit up. He took her face in both his hands and pressed an open-mouthed kiss to her lips. He stepped closer and pulled her into a tight embrace. Marlene dropped the crutches and slipped her arms around his neck. He kissed her again, deeper and more urgent. There was nothing tentative or reserved about his actions.

Marlene's heartbeat picked up. Her body tingled from head to toe. Brady continued to kiss her senseless. When they finally broke apart, she steadied herself by holding his shoulders. His passion threw her off-balance and would've had the same effect with or without her broken leg.

"Wow," she said, unable to come up with anything else. "Was that a yes? Will you stay tonight?"

Brady smiled and nodded. "Let's take it slow, though, because I really don't want to ruin this. God help me, this is about to sound cheesy as hell, but it's the absolute truth. All I want to do is fall asleep with you in my arms."

Marlene's heart swelled. "You've got yourself a deal."

Ellen cradled the red coffee mug in both hands and sipped. She kept it close to her face and peered over the top at Marlene, one eyebrow raised.

"What is it?" Marlene asked.

Ellen sighed. "Did you and Brady sleep together? Something's different about you." Faith came by and leaned her body against Ellen. Ellen petted her head.

"We didn't have sex if that's what you mean."

"What else would I mean?"

"We slept in the same bed, like actually fell asleep."

"Marlene, be careful with your heart. Don't rush into anything. What if your memory comes back and you can't stand the sight of him? That would be awful for you both." She lifted the mug to her lips.

"Did you know I was supposed to move to San Diego in May?"

Ellen started coughing. She set down the coffee and pounded on her chest. "What?"

Marlene's shoulders slumped. "Damn. So you didn't."

Ellen's mouth opened then closed. She shook her head. "Why would you keep that a secret? Please tell me you're not really leaving."

"I sold the house," Marlene said, her voice sounding small and hollow to her own ears. Tears burned at the back of her eyes. "I'm so confused." She pinched the bridge of her nose. "I grew up in this house. I raised Noah in this house, and I always thought"—she swallowed and sucked in a breath—"that I would raise my own babies here, too. I must have been so sad."

Recognition shined in Ellen's eyes. "You've been obsessed with purging things lately. It makes sense now. You were getting rid of everything you weren't taking with you." Ellen took a shaky breath. "You don't need to leave just because you sold the house. Stay with me, Justin, and the kids until you decide your next move."

"The thing is, while I can't remember any of the details, I can sense how determined I was to make this happen. It wasn't a knee-jerk decision. It was carefully planned out, right down to not telling anyone my real plans."

"I don't want you to go." Ellen dabbed at the corner of her eye, keeping the tears at bay. "But I understand."

Marlene's brows creased. "I'm sorry, Ellen."

Ellen waved the apology away. "And here I was worried Brady would break you. Did you tell him yet?"

Marlene shook her head. "I wanted to. I tried a few times, but I chickened out. He's taking me to the Winter Festival tonight. I'm going to do it then."

"You should. Don't lead him on."

Marlene nodded. Ellen slumped in her chair and rested her face in her hands.

Chapter Seventeen

B rady pulled into Red Ridge Park and cut the engine. He hopped out of the truck, practically bouncing to the passenger side door. The cold night air washed over him, warmth tingling throughout his body in spite of the chilly temperature. Winter Festival had always been one of their things. Every year he and Marlene would ice skate on the frozen pond, drink hot apple cider, and eat s'mores by the bonfire. Of course, there would be no skating for Marlene tonight, but the fact that a "them" existed was enough for him to crack a huge grin.

He helped Marlene out of the vehicle, handing her the crutches from behind her seat. The lights from the parking lot cast a warm glow down on them. They moved toward the crowd. She flashed an uneasy smile.

"What's up?" he asked.

"Nothing." Her voice came out more high-pitched than normal. "Why?"

He cocked his head and met her gaze. "Did you remember something?"

"No." She rubbed her arm.

"You seem...distracted."

"I'm fine." She touched his shoulder. "Really, I swear."

When they reached the entrance, Brady paid for admission. The place was swarming with people. Couples, both old and young, and families with kids of all ages milled around.

The scent of sugary goodness wafted through the air and filled Brady's nose. His mouth watered. He spotted Murray's food truck close by. Marlene tilted her head in its direction. "Donuts and cider, here we come," she said, keeping her eyes on the destination.

"Works for me." Brady scratched the back of his neck as he followed her lead. Why wouldn't she look at him?

They placed an order at the window and carried their sweet treats to a nearby, empty picnic table.

Marlene bit into a donut, her eyes nearly rolling into the back of her head. "They're still warm. Mmm."

The sound that escaped her mouth conjured images that had nothing to do with donuts. He shifted in his seat and took a bite of his own. Yes, it was delicious, but when his gaze dropped to her lips, he was willing to bet she tasted way better. He pushed away the thought, trying to ignore the blood rushing south in his body.

When his mind cleared, he studied Marlene's uninjured leg bobbing up and down and her hands twisting in her lap. Could she be nervous? On their first date, he had taken Marlene to the movies. In the darkness of the theater, her fingers fidgeted this way and that. He learned early on that she didn't verbalize her emotions, but he could read them like a book if he paid enough attention.

He wrapped his hands around the insulated paper cup, steam from the hot cider rising into the night. When they were warm, he reached for Marlene's.

"Are you cold?" he asked.

She shook her head.

"Come on." He stood.

"Where are we going?" She angled her head up toward him, her hazel eyes bright with curiosity.

"Well, we can't ice skate, and I don't want you walking around too much on these crutches. It's slippery out."

"Oh." Marlene dropped her gaze to the pavement between them. "You want to leave? I'm sorry I'm a lousy date."

He lifted her chin with his forefinger. "No. I want to do something we've never done before." He led her to the curb where a line formed for horse-drawn carriage rides and stood behind the last couple.

Her eyes widened and she let out a short burst of laughter. "You hate these things. Forced romance, you used to tell me."

"But you always liked them." He pressed his lips to the back of her hand. "I'm trying to show you I'm a changed man." He winked.

"I loved the idea of them. I've never actually been on one before."

The next carriage pulled up beside them. "Yes, and I'm fixing that." Brady scooped Marlene up in his arms and she squealed, losing a crutch in the process. He placed her in the seat and handed her the crutches. He ran around to the other side and climbed up, settling so close their thighs touched.

"Good evening," the driver said.

"Hello," Brady and Marlene said in unison.

"Would you like one loop around the grounds or two?" he asked.

Brady gave Marlene a sidelong glance, one corner of his mouth kicking up. "Two please," he said.

"No problem." The man turned around and gave a light flick of the reins. The carriage started rolling.

Brady draped an arm over Marlene's shoulders. She leaned into him, pressing against his side. He kissed the top of her head. They plodded along in silence.

One of the things he loved about their relationship was their ability to enjoy the presence of each other. No words necessary. His heart banged around in his chest. He wasn't a particularly lucky man under normal circumstances, but tonight, it was as if he had won the lottery. "I'll admit this isn't terrible," he said.

Marlene faced him. Their gazes locked. He leaned in and when she didn't back away, he brought his lips to hers. "You make me so damn happy." Their foreheads pressed together.

Marlene closed her eyes a brief moment. She placed her soft hands on his cheeks. "I'm afraid to remember why we went wrong. I don't want to lose us." She planted a fierce, unapologetic kiss on him, claiming him in a way that set every nerve ending on fire. Her tongue darted into his mouth and brushed across his. She tasted of sweet apples and sugar, filling him with love he had once believed to be gone.

"Stay with me tonight, Brady," she whispered before she caught his mouth with hers again.

"I'm yours," he said between kisses. "Always will be."

Chapter Eighteen

M arlene almost told Brady about the move during the festival. The little voice inside her head screamed *Do it. Do it now!* At least a dozen times, and yet, she failed to follow through. She opted to kiss him instead. More than once.

Here they were back at her house, as she requested. They had let Faith out and fed her, and now they were headed upstairs. Marlene passed the guest bedroom and continued down the hallway.

"Where are you going?" Brady asked from behind her.

She stopped to glance at him over her shoulder. "To our room."

"Ours?" His voice filled with emotion.

She nodded and pivoted sideways to look at him. "Ever since you brought me home from the hospital, the idea of sleeping in there without you didn't feel right. That's the truth."

His throat worked.

She continued to the bedroom. Brady went to her side of the bed and propped up pillows for her leg, like he had all the other nights. Except she wanted tonight to be different.

Marlene rested her crutches against the nightstand and eased herself down, grabbing Brady's shirt as she went. She pulled him toward her and kissed him like she may never get the chance again. And, who knew? Maybe she wouldn't.

"Marlene," Brady breathed. "You're killing me. Anymore and I won't be able to hold back."

She loosened her grip on the fabric, sliding her hands under the hem, grazing her fingers across his bare skin. "Please don't." Her mouth brushed his, once then again. She nibbled on his lower lip, eliciting a deep, rich groan that sent a jolt of pleasure through her body. "Because I don't want you to."

Chapter Nineteen

B rady breezed into work and set a coffee on Scott's desk. "Morning, bro."

"Hey." Scott stopped typing and crossed his arms, his lips splitting into a smile. "Someone has a spring in their step this morning. How's Marlene?"

"She's great." Brady sat down and started his computer. Thinking about last night gave him chills.

He grabbed a thick stack of invoices from the box on the corner of his desk and entered them into the system. Afterward, he took a call with a customer and scheduled an oil delivery. His cell buzzed in his pocket.

Marlene: "I'm at Murray's. Can we talk?"

Brady held the phone further away from his face like an elderly man unable to read the words. How did she get to Murray's? She couldn't drive with a broken leg. He sighed. While he had been sitting on cloud nine all morning, she probably spent the same stretch of time freaking out about what had happened between them.

He had zero regrets. He loved her, and he would reassure her that all would be fine. He wasn't going anywhere.

Brady: "Sure. Be over in a minute."

"I'll be back in a few," Brady said to Scott as he rose to his feet. He tried to tell himself everything was okay, even as a knot formed in his stomach.

"What's wrong?" Scott asked, his brows furrowed.

"Not sure. Marlene's at the coffee shop, and she wants to talk."

"Maybe she couldn't stand being apart from you for all of two hours." Scott laughed, but his pinched expression said otherwise.

Brady took a deep breath. "Let's hope so."

Scott's lips pressed into a thin line. "Remember what we talked about. Don't let her go without a fight."

Brady gave a single, firm nod and walked out the door. As he crossed the street, he spotted Marlene. She sat on a bench in front of the café, with a blank stare, no drink in her hand, no pastries either.

His shoulders tensed as he plopped down beside her. Before she spoke, he took one slender hand in both of his. "Whatever you're about to say isn't going to drive me away, Marlene. Don't be worried about us. I'll show you. We're going to be fine."

"I'm leaving, Brady. I'm moving to California in May."

His jaw dropped open. She would never leave this town. She was the one constant he counted on in Mistport. "No, you're not." He shook his head. No way.

"I didn't mean to give you false hope. I'm not even sure why I decided to do it, but I made the decision before the accident and I owe it to myself to figure out why." Marlene might as well have torn his heart out of his chest and stomped all over it.

"Tell me you're kidding." He ground his teeth together. "I thought we were getting another chance."

Her gaze met his. "We could. Come with me."

His pulse hammered in his ears. "What?"

"You always wanted me to broaden my horizons. I'm going to do it, and I want you by my side. What do you say?"

He laced his hands behind his head and pulled. "Why didn't you tell me yesterday? How long have you known, Marlene? Did your memory come back?"

"I tried, but I wimped out. We were having such a wonderful night. I didn't want to ruin it. I was afraid you wouldn't want to come with me." She slumped forward. "You don't. I can tell."

"Whether or not I want to is irrelevant. I can't. I promised Scott and Trina that I would help them. They're depending on me."

"Just until the babies are born, right?" She leaned toward him.

Brady gave a small shake of his head as emptiness washed over him. "For much longer than that. A few years."

He never got around to telling Marlene about the full-time job he would start in September. The one that provided affordable childcare for Scott and Trina, so their business would continue to thrive, and they could raise their children with stability that Brady and Scott never had growing up. He refused to let them down.

She stared at her hands, expelling a long sigh. "I understand. You need to take care of your family." She nodded, a sad smile emerging on her face. "If anyone would get that, it would be me."

For the first time in his life, he was trying to stay put. The irony of the situation placed his heart in a vice. All the times he came to Marlene, telling her Noah was fine without her, and that she should do whatever she wanted, it was all a load of crap. He had pressured her for doing the right thing for her brother, just as he was doing for his now.

He deserved this. Karma sucked.

A silver Honda pulled up with an Uber sign in the window. "That's my ride," Marlene said. "Thank you for helping me after the accident.

I'm sorry I hid the truth for a little while." She removed her hand from his grasp and headed for the car. She opened the door and glanced back at him. "For what it's worth, Brady, I love you."

The bittersweet taste of her words slammed into him as she drove off. She had his heart again, and she was taking it with her.

Chapter Twenty

M arlene stared out the car window, her hand pressed to her chest as if it would keep her heart from breaking into tiny pieces. It didn't. She should've been used to losing everyone she loved. There never seemed to be an alternate ending for her.

She stepped out of the car and glared up at the house. The happy memories she recalled, some with her parents, others after they passed, seemed tainted by the horrible reality that Noah and Tracy were no longer around either. The weight of missing them pressed on her shoulders, threatening to push her to the ground.

Good riddance.

She hobbled inside with her head hung low.

When she closed the door behind her, Faith greeted her in her usual butt-wagging way. Tears welled in her eyes. At least she still had Faith. The dog scampered off, knocking over a pile of empty boxes Marlene assembled earlier in the day.

Marlene re-stacked all but one. She carried the remaining box over to the entertainment center, opening one of the drawers and tossing old DVDs and Blu-Rays in. She streamed all her movies now, so she wouldn't need to haul these across the country. She would ask Ellen to help her with donations, since carrying stuff with a broken leg would be a challenge.

She grabbed the box top, but when she went to cover the box, a DVD in the pile caught her attention. A piece of paper had been slipped under the sleeve, her own handwriting scrawled across it: *Noah and Tracy's Wedding, August 15, 2016.*

She swallowed the golf ball that lodged in her throat. She simultaneously wanted to watch it and set it on fire. With her heart pounding in her chest, she turned on the DVD player and stuck the disk in.

She sunk to the floor and hit play.

Noah stood on the beach, just steps away from the house. Another man waited beside him, who must have been the officiant.

"Hurry up, Marlene. My best man should be standing next to me when my bride comes out." Noah waved an arm at the camera.

Marlene let out a short burst of laughter as she swiped at the tears streaming down her cheeks. That sounded like something Noah would say to her. Video Marlene joined Noah a second later, wearing the emerald dress she remembered from the photo.

"Will you quit crying? Best men aren't supposed to cry," Noah said.

"Stop being an ass." Video Marlene punched him in the arm. "I'm just happy for you."

With her heart in her throat, present day Marlene observed every last minute of the recording. From Faith carrying out the wedding bands on a pillow tied to her back, to Noah and Tracy exchanging vows, the ceremony was simple and nothing short of perfect.

Her chest squeezed. Bits of the day drifted back to Marlene's mind. She envisioned the three of them on the back deck. "Congratulations to the happiest couple I've ever known," Marlene had said to the two of them, placing an envelope in Tracy's hand. "In case you two want to go on a honeymoon. If you don't, save it for something good."

Tracy had pulled Marlene in for a tight hug. "I always wanted a sister. I'm glad it's you."

Noah hugged her next. "Thanks, sis. We'll put it toward a down payment for a house."

Marlene swallowed. The doorbell rang. "Just a minute." She opened the door to find Brady on the front stoop. She said nothing.

"What's wrong?" he asked.

She raised an eyebrow. "Seriously?"

He nodded. "Sorry. Stupid question. I think we should talk."

Marlene turned and headed for the living room. She didn't invite him in, but she didn't shut the door in his face. He followed.

She slumped into a chair. "When was Noah and Tracy's accident?"

Brady frowned, picking up the DVD case, studying the wedding date. "A few days after they got married. I don't know the details since I was away and we were already..." He sighed, clasping his hand over the back of his neck.

"I tried to send them on a trip, but they insisted on a staycation. They were saving for a place of their own." She inhaled deep and blew the breath out slow. "I really wish they had taken me up on my offer."

"I've been thinking." Brady sat on the couch. He leaned forward, resting his forearms on his knees. "One of the reasons we fell apart was because neither of us would compromise."

"No?" Marlene asked.

"You wanted to stay in Mistport and have babies. I wanted to live abroad, and then settle down in an area of our choosing to start a family. There was no in-between." He raked his hands over his face. "I don't want to make the same mistake twice."

Marlene hugged herself. She didn't want to lose him either. "So, what now?"

He angled toward her and looked her in the eye. "I meant it when I said I love you, but I don't want you to stay for me."

Marlene's eyebrows creased. Her heart rate sped up as he crossed the space between them and kneeled in front of her. "I want you to go to California, and I want us to be together even though I can't leave for a while."

Heaviness settled in her stomach. "The last time we tried a long distance relationship it didn't end well."

"And this can be our opportunity to get it right." He cupped her face with both hands and pressed a kiss to her lips. Heat flashed through her body as his tongue tangled with hers. He wrapped his arms around her. She melted into his body.

Marlene didn't want to abandon their relationship. There was a chance they could make it work, but they would never know if she wasn't willing to try.

Brady broke the kiss and met Marlene's gaze. "In a few years, once I've fulfilled my commitment to Scott and Trina, I will follow you anywhere, as long as you'll let me. What do you say?"

Marlene pushed his dark hair away from his forehead and bit her bottom lip. "Second chances are rare. Let's take advantage of the one we've got."

Brady hugged her so hard she squeaked. "I won't let you down. I promise."

She pressed her lips to his. "I'm counting on it."

EPILOGUE

Six months later...

Brady shut his apartment door with one foot and tossed his keys on the table. He hung his coat and kicked off his shoes. His cell phone vibrated.

A Skype window flashed on the screen, *Marlene Martin calling* displayed front and center. Brady grinned and pressed the *Answer with video* button.

She was on-time, as always. They had a standing call every other day at eleven at night. The distance didn't tear them apart as they had feared. They talked often and didn't shy from making plans for the future. Life was good.

"Hey babe." Brady said. "How was your day?"

The corners of her mouth turned up. "Excellent. I landed the new client I told you about last week. Paige, Sierra, and I went to happy hour to celebrate and I just got home. How was yours?"

"Congratulations. I never doubted you would. My day was decent. Watched the triplets for a few hours so Scott and Trina could do date night. They seemed thrilled to get out for a bit."

"I cannot wait to see how you handle three babies at once." Marlene shook her head. Warmth radiated in Brady's chest.

"Thanksgiving will be here before you know it, and then we'll be together again. Prepare to be impressed by..." Brady kept the phone at arm's length. He rested one foot on a chair and propped a hand on his hip, his chin held high. In a deep voice, he said, "Super Uncle."

She burst into laughter. "You gave yourself a superhero title? Do you own a cape, too?"

He smirked. "No, but if you wanted to pick one up for me, I wouldn't hate on it."

"You're ridiculous," she said.

"I'm excited. I can't wait for you to come back for Thanksgiving. I may have to challenge Ellen to a duel to win your time, but I will do it. You mark my words."

Marlene's eyebrows rose. "You are really hyper tonight."

"I am. I have the most incredible news that I can't hold back any longer. Trina's mom announced that she's retiring at the end of the year so she can spend more time with her grandbabies. Do you know what that means?"

Marlene covered her mouth with her hand. "Are you saying what I think you're saying?"

Brady nodded. "Soon, I'll be a free man. Do you still want me to join you in San Diego?"

Marlene's eyes blazed with emotion. Her throat worked. "I thought you'd never ask."

Marlene loved living in San Diego, but being apart from Brady for several months had been rough. Bits and pieces of her memories returned to her here and there, but none of the bad ones held enough weight to ruin the beautiful thing she had going with Brady.

They talked all the time, but it wasn't enough. She couldn't wait to be in his arms again.

Her flight landed at JFK without incident. She grabbed her luggage from the baggage claim and wheeled it to the ground transportation area outside. Following Brady's instructions from earlier in the day, she pulled out her phone to text him that she had arrived at their meeting spot.

Her fingers flew over the screen, but before she hit send, a shrill whistle cut through the air. She glanced around and spotted Brady in the distance. His red pickup truck stood out in a sea of black cars with tinted windows. Drivers waited outside their respective vehicles and held up white signs with names printed on them. To Marlene's surprise, Brady was doing the same thing.

She rolled her bags behind her as she moved in his direction, eyeing "Marlene Martin" written in bright green ink. "Um, what's with the sign? Did you think I wouldn't recognize you? It hasn't been that long." His face brightened as she drew near, sending her pulse into overdrive.

A mischievous grin crept up on his face and he flipped the card over. Two words stared back at Marlene in bold red ink, followed by a question mark:

MARRY ME?

Marlene's jaw dropped open. She froze on the sidewalk. "Is this for real?"

Brady reached into his pocket and closed the distance between them. "I never want to be away from you again." He went down on one knee and opened a tiny box, revealing an engagement ring with a platinum band, a large diamond in the center and two smaller ones on either side.

Marlene's vision blurred as wetness pooled in her eyes.

"I always wished we would find our way back to each other. Life is short, and I don't want to waste another minute without the love of my life. You will always be my one and only. Marry me, Marlene."

She gaped at him. A moment passed and still she said nothing.

Brady's forehead wrinkled. "Too soon? I'll wait for you Marlene. I'll give you as long as you need." He rose to his feet, his cheeks turning red.

Marlene grabbed his hand. "That's not it at all."

"Then what is it?" He searched her eyes for the answer.

She slipped a thick silver band off her thumb and held it up. "I planned to ask you first. See?" An inscription on the inside read: *Forever yours, Marlene*.

Brady stood speechless, his eyes widened.

"Brady Miller, will you be my husband?" Her heart pounded in her chest.

He laughed. "Yes," he answered, crushing her to his body.

She yelped. "Careful. I don't want to drop your ring." He loosened his hold. She took his left hand and slipped it on his finger.

Brady freed the other ring from its velvet box and placed it on her finger. The drivers waiting for their passengers cheered and clapped.

"Kiss her!" someone yelled.

Brady took Marlene in his arms and kissed her like his life depended on it. She returned the fire in equal measure.

Life was a series of unexpected twists and turns. Marlene never would have guessed that getting hit by a car could bring her to this moment. It had led her back to the person she shouldn't have lost to begin with, and for this, she was grateful.

THE END

About the Author

Melissa J. Crispin loves to mix things up by writing YA, Fantasy, and Romance. A fintech professional by day, a novelist by night, she pursues her passion for writing in her hometown of Stamford, Connecticut. When she's not working, she spends her time reading, listening to audiobooks, and binging TV shows that her two teenage kids say she's too old to watch.

Visit Melissa's website at www.melissajcrispin.com or connect with her online:

Facebook: facebook.com/melissajcrispinauthor

Instagram: @MelissaJCrispin

Twitter: @MelissaJCrispin

Also By Melissa J. Crispin

The Crimson Curse

Collide